For Dad

WITHDRAWN

www.mascotbooks.com

Go Down the Mountain

©2019 Meredith Battle. All Rights Reserved. No part of this publication may be reproduced, stored in a retrieval system or transmitted in any form by any means electronic, mechanical, or photocopying, recording or otherwise without the permission of the author.

Cover art by Antonia Walker, *Apple Orchard Rappahannock*

This is a work of fiction. Names, characters, businesses, places, events, and incidents are either the products of the author's imagination or used in a fictitious manner. Any resemblance to actual persons, living or dead, or actual events is purely coincidental.

For more information, please contact:
Mascot Books
620 Herndon Parkway, Suite 320
Herndon, VA 20170
info@mascotbooks.com

Library of Congress Control Number: 2018905814

CPSIA Code: PROPM0918A
ISBN-13: 978-1-64307-013-1

Printed in the United States

Go Down the Mountain

Mountain

MEREDITH BATTLE

| PROLOGUE |

My dear Amelia, I raised you up to believe the wrong man was your daddy. I let him believe it too, long as he put food on the table and a roof over your head. But ever since your real daddy passed, my fingers have been itching to put the truth to paper. I won't tell you what kind of man your daddy was. I'll let my story do that and you be the judge. I won't name him either, least not till the end. I'll bet you a stack of Liberty half dollars that, before the end rolls around, you'll know him without my telling you.

You won't be set to read this for a long while seeing as how you've only got three years on this earth. But when the time comes and you lay eyes on these pages, you ought to know there are some downright ugly secrets in this story about your own kin and your mama to boot. There's cursing, folks getting it on and entirely too much killing. You might not want to read the worst of it, like how our own country's government stole folks' land then locked them away for their troubles, or how the mama who nursed you through whooping cough once lured a man to a grisly death.

Still, I think a girl should know where she came from, even if it's not all pretty. Now the mountains -- there's pretty for you. There was enough beauty in our mountains and the Hollow to make up for a world of warts. The life I knew there got disappeared by the government. That doesn't matter. It's as much a part of you as all the rest of it.

| A DEAL THAT WOULD MAKE THE DEVIL FLINCH |

My Mama named me Ada Anabelle after her own self, which is just about the last name I would have chosen if she'd given baby me a say in it. I guess the joke was on her since, soon as I could talk, she didn't much care to claim me as her own. Daddy did us all a favor and took to calling me Busy Bee on account of he said I was always buzzing around looking for what trouble I could get into. The Bee part stuck and that's what Hollow folks called me.

The whole Hollow was named after us, after Daddy's people anyway -- Livingston. It was the Livingstons who built the first houses there more than a hundred years ago. They must have thought they'd found Eden when they first laid eyes on the place. Black woods set so close the light was green, violets underfoot, streams cold enough to shock even in summer.

In all those years between the first Livingstons and me, only the chestnut trees changed. They got done in by blight when I was an ankle biter -- the same year cousin Samuel went moonlight coon hunting dead drunk and stumbled his fool self to a broken neck at the bottom of Thompson's Gorge. Put your nose up close to their trunks and you might have thought an angry bear had its way with them. They were all torn up with gashes where the blight's sores split their bark. But even dead those trees stayed standing. I used to pretend they tracked who came and went from the Hollow, good as any hired guards. Turns out they couldn't keep the bad away.

I passed by those trees plenty but, when I first laid eyes on Miles Everheart, I still hadn't gone farther than to Luray with my Daddy and to Richmond to see Mama's family. I reckon that was why I was so eaten up with need to be with Miles. He wasn't much older than me, and there he was about to cross the country and see places I could only visit in books. Being with him felt like maybe I could claim a little part of his adventure for myself.

Now's as good a time as any to tell you I have two beaus in this story. There was Miles. I'm just about to spell out how I fell for him fast as a rock tossed off a ledge. The second one, Torch, started out as a boy who grew up with me on the mountain. We were so much alike we could have been that pair of Siamese twins from England I read about in the paper once, except instead of being attached by an ass cheek, we shared one mind. I'll get to Torch in a spell.

Miles was a government photographer come from Washington to take pictures of the Hollow for an office called the Resettlement Administration. His boss told him his photographs would make the case for helping poor people down on their luck. He believed it and so did I when he told me. It's easy to look back now and see us as fools. I'll remind you that, until a few years ago, we'd never heard of the government stealing land away from anybody -- at least not white folks.

Miles spent a month in the Hollow before he got his next assignment. Those weeks shine in my memory. I had a fondness for him that was fierce at its beginning. The first day we met at MacArthur's Store he offered me five dollars to show him the Hollow. That was a whole hell of a lot of money to me so I agreed even though common sense told me leading a city man around was going to be more than five dollars' worth of trouble. I made him pay me half up front and came up with a plan to ditch him. I took him straight up the mountain on the steepest, rockiest trail I knew. Hard as I tried to shake him, Miles stayed with me the whole way to the top. I'm still stumped about how he managed it. He slipped and slid so much in his city shoes you'd have thought he was a newborn fawn strapped into a pair of ice skates. He never complained once though, not even when he fell on his ass in the briar patch I went out of my way to take him through.

I agreed to meet him at MacArthur's again the next day. I noticed right away he'd gone and bought himself some sensible boots and jeans that would stand up to a few briar pricks. I also noticed he was handsome in a fine-boned, citified way. He looked painted with one color, a sort of hazel all over, except for his lips which were a bubblegum pink and seemed an advertisement to kiss him, which I did later that day. It wasn't long before he was nothing but hungry hands and eyes whenever it was just us two. He had a nervous air about him that got soothed when he was alone with me. I liked having such an effect.

We laid together in the orchard the day he left the Hollow. He took my picture and sent it to me months later. In it, my skin was the silver of mercury. My black hair twisted wildly as Medusa's snakes. My gray eyes teased his camera. He said he carried a print of that same photo in his bag. I liked to think of him looking at me, even from far away.

I'm glad I haven't forgotten that last day on the mountain with him. Even the grass remembered us for a while, pressed flat by two bodies, bruised by our romp before he left to go back to the world. Maybe I shouldn't mention anything to you about me being with a man who wasn't my husband. A proper mother, like the ones here in the city, wouldn't. God knows there's never been much proper about me. I was educated. Mama was the Hollow school teacher and she saw to that. But I've always used words I shouldn't, like goddamn and bastard, and I let my heart get so hot it boils over. Mothers and girls never had much use for me, but boys and men always seemed eager to see me happy.

After the snakes killed Daddy, there were plenty of boys, men even, who came around with apple butter jars or scratched and bleeding arms full of the best huckleberries from the thistly patch up on goat's trail. If you want to know, I kissed a few of them. But Miles was the first man I ever laid with. I'm not ashamed to say the love I had with him, wrestled to its end in the cool shade of the apple trees, was sweeter to me than the best whiskey. Yes, your mama has tasted whiskey too. I hope you won't take it too hard if, in the course of reading these pages, you find out I'm not as ladylike as you might have hoped.

His boss at the Resettlement Administration aimed to make Miles a happy carpetbagger -- Alabama and Arkansas, then the Midwest and on to California (where I'd heard the land was so rich, a strawberry seed spit into the dirt would bloom into a plant in a week's time). It satisfied him to know his pictures would do good, that Uncle Sam would use them to make the case to the American taxpayers for helping folks down on their luck. I got my first letter from him when he settled in down south. When I looked up from those hushed pages, I was wading through a sea of white Alabama cotton alongside Negro pickers, black as wet fieldstone, glory-to-God hymns rising from their work-wasted bodies like steam. The wicked Dixie sun prickled our skin, stung our eyes with sweat. Prickly cotton plants tore at my clothes, jealous lovers, greedy for another touch. I was sweet on Miles before he left. Soon as I read that letter, I was sure I'd fallen whole hog in love.

When it came time for me to write back, I was afraid my letter would be the end of it. Mama had us write plenty of practice letters at school, but my letter to Miles was only the second one I'd ever mailed. The first was for a school project. Mama found us a group of pen pals at a school in Washington, D.C. and I wrote to mine about the dead, bloated deer that exploded all over Daddy when he hit it with a stick because he was too drunk to think better of it. Everybody in class got a return letter but me, so I'd come to believe I wasn't cut out for correspondence.

I steered clear of dead, rotting things and wrote about my feelings for Miles instead. Mama always said I put too much stock in feelings. She called it a sickness and said I ought to hope for a cure, but back then I would have picked death over living without someone who could make the letters light up when they said my name. Miles did that in the beginning. So do you, sweet girl, every time you say mama.

My Mama was healthy as a horse on spring grass, free from the kind of sentiment that ailed me. I suspected it was because I'd been such a calamity as a daughter. She had to harden her heart to weather the disappointment. I used to try to change myself to please her. I only succeeded once in a while and, when I did, her goodwill flitted away again quick as a hummingbird.

There was some ugly business between Mama and me the day I got that first letter from Miles. I remember because I was all goo-goo eyed after I read my name written in his hand and not at all ready for what came next. A state man called Rowler was the cause of it. He came by our place and said the state had given our land to Uncle Sam for a park. We were to be out in five months or be considered at odds with the law.

Mama told him we'd sell. Our land was worth fifteen dollars an acre, she said. She made a big speech about how we wouldn't take any less for it. While she talked, Rowler looked me up and down and licked his lips like I was a slice of scrapple fresh from the frying pan. He was the kind of husky white man who had a layer of pasty fat on him from sitting on his ass in a desk chair, his cheeks flushed pink from sneaking sips of whiskey. His brown mustache twitched even when he wasn't talking, until I thought it might jump off his face and scurry into a hole in the floorboards.

He told Mama we wouldn't get squat since Daddy's people never filed papers with the county courthouse. I figured as much. Daddy always said the Livingstons didn't need papers when a handshake and a man's word would do. Seems like we didn't need a deed when the whole goddamned

Hollow was named for us.

Mama was fit to be tied. Rowler grinned a pleased-with-himself grin. Then he tried to make a deal with Mama that would have made the devil flinch.

"Your girl looks like she sure could keep a man warm at night," he said. "If she had a notion to show me some kindness, I'd see to it you get one of the houses the government's built for your people, down on Resettlement Road." I took a sideways glance at Mama and saw she looked confused. Rowler must have seen it too because he spoke plain as he could and still lay claim to a shred of decency. "It'll take some time with your daughter to bring out my generous nature. Without it, you're on your own."

Mama went mute. He told her to take some time to think it over. He'd be back.

Me and Mama had a whopping row after he left. I was mad as hell at her for not telling him off soon as he opened his mouth about me. She said didn't I know what shock was and how could she be expected to have her wits about her after what he'd asked. But when I pressed her to swear she'd set him straight the next time, she wouldn't do it. She just kept on about how we were in a heap of trouble if we got kicked off our land with no money to show for it.

"Just flirt with him a little until we get one of those houses," she said. "Let him think he's got a chance."

I lost my temper. "He wants more than that," I said. "Are you planning to whore out your own daughter?" She gave me two good smacks across the face and that was the end of it. Mama and I were always oil and water. Rowler shaking us up did more harm than good. He was after me to lay with him and all Mama could do was chew it over. I wasn't a nervous girl, but I was near about having kittens over it. I had to sneak a sip or two of white mule (that's what us mountain folks called whiskey) to get to sleep that night.

| BAD TIMES COMING |

Rowler or no, I was doe-eyed that fall. I thought I knew the season by heart, but that year it was foggy with memories. I saw Miles in the jonquil patch I used for daydreaming, on the deer trail to my friend Ruth's place, behind stalks of ripened corn. I would kiss my letters to him and pray that they could bear the love I had felt for him skin-to-skin that summer, until the day we locked lips over the same spot of earth again.

On the way to the Ruth and Peter's corn shucking, I was giddy with love and didn't take care to check the temperature of Mama's mood. I told Mama she should send Rowler a letter and warn him to leave us be. He left a card with his address, so it would be easy enough to do. "Daddy would do it," I said. "He would have told that son of a bitch what he could do with himself soon as my name came out of his mouth."

"Your Daddy's the one who got us into this fix -- ignorant mountain man too stupid to set foot in a courthouse and sign off on what's his." Mama was from Richmond and always looking down her nose at mountain folk, even the one she picked to marry.

Then Mama started in trying to sell me on Rowler again. Things went downhill from there. He was good looking, she said, had a government job. I could do worse. I told her if she thought I was going to ride off into the sunset with that bastard she had another thing coming. She said we'd starve while I sat on my high horse. She swung us right around for home. I had to all but throw myself at her feet to get her to change her mind and head back to the party.

Sometimes, if I was shamefaced enough to satisfy her, she'd go easy on me. Other times, it just got her more worked up. That night it worked in my favor. Thank the Lord above because, in the end, not even Mama's hissy fit could ruin that night.

There must have been fifty people at Ruth's. Ruth Evers was my stand-in mama. She and Torch were the only two friends I had. From a distance she had the look of Aphrodite, risen from sea foam with pale skin and flaxen hair that fell in soft curls. Close up, she disappointed. Her delicate features crowded together, drawn with too small a hand on her broad face. But her looks were no matter to me. She was a kind of goddess anyway -- of wild and helpless things. She mothered me when I needed it and she cared for folks on the mountain like a mother would. She was known across four hollows for making good medicine from our mountain plants. The tea she made with deadly nightshade could cure a whole host of ills.

The night of the shucking, Ruth crowded her table with the Limoges china set her mama passed down. It had little pink roses that trailed across a milky white background. I'd never seen anything finer. Ruth's daddy hired himself out as a stone mason all of one summer to earn the nineteen dollars it cost to buy it from the Sears and Roebuck catalog. He gave it to Ruth's mama on their twentieth wedding anniversary. Sometimes Ruth let me take it out of the sideboard to admire it. I liked to trace the flowers with my pointing finger.

The food that night was as first rate as the plates. The serving dishes were piled with mountains of spare ribs fried up from a hog slaughtered the day before, scrapple, corn pone, boiled potatoes and stewed apples. There was a pyramid of warm biscuits on a platter, attended by a pitcher of milk and sausage gravy. There were bowls of apple butter and canned peaches. Coffee stewed on the wood stove in a copper pot. I filled my plate so full I couldn't see its rose pattern until I'd eaten a whole biscuit.

Once the food was eaten up and everyone turned in their plates, Ruth sent the crowd to the barn to get started shucking. She grabbed me by my back pocket on my way out the door. She motioned for me to follow her to the kitchen, where she whispered, "What you so glum for, Honey Bee? You ain't let two words out of that bear trap you got for a mouth all night. You and your Mama get into a row?"

I told her begging Mama to let me come to the party had taken the stuffing out of me. "I'm having the best night just the same Ruth," I said.

"Lying's a sin, sweet girl," Ruth said. "I don't normally cotton to whiskey drinking, but I reckon a swig or two won't do you no harm. Get on out to the barn and get you a drink. Forget about your Mama."

Ruth gave me a hug that soothed me more than whiskey could. Her hair smelled like snakeroot, probably from some medicine she'd been cooking up earlier. Times like those, I wished God had picked Ruth to be my mama.

By the time I got to the barn, a few of the men had taken up the fiddle and the mouth harp and two red-ear cheaters had downed their first drinks. We had a corn shucking tradition that the man who unwrapped a red ear got a swig of the farmer's whiskey. Ruth's husband Peter bought bonded liquor all the way from Kentucky. It tasted better than anything we made in mountain stills. You've never seen so many red ears of corn in your life. Peter was a good spirit so he never did call them on it.

The corn got shucked in spite of all the drinking. Then people pushed the chairs up against the barn walls and paired off for dancing in the middle. I didn't dare dance in front of Mama. Something about the heat still in her eyes told me it'd be best not to. I was careful not to bump the barn door open wider when I eased through the crack in it, so she didn't see me leave.

I found three of the men outside passing a quart jug of white mule. They were singing ballads and carrying on to an oil lantern that had grown so tired of their nonsense it could only turn out a weak glimmer. Torch was there with Red Monroe and Ruth's husband Peter.

 Torch and Red made a harebrained pair when they were together, I can tell you. Torch started out like a brother to me, except when he was around Red sometimes I didn't care to claim him. I'll get to him a few pages from now. His troubles take some time to tell, so I can't fit them in here.

Red was a good ten years older than Torch. I guess that made him somewhere around thirty. Don't be confused into thinking Red was any more mature for his age. He had himself a devilish nature that got him into plenty of trouble. When he was fifteen, he fell out of a scrawny pine his horny self climbed to get a look at a couple of girls splashing around Miller's swimming hole in the altogether. He cracked his left hip bone and he had an old man's limp because of it.

You may have guessed from his name that Red had hair the color of fire. I'd heard it said redheads couldn't be trusted. Daddy told me that was superstition folks carried in their suitcases from whatever old country they were born in. Daddy didn't go in much for superstition. I didn't usually either, but Red did a damned fine job proving this one to be true. When his mama died, he cut off her long silver hair and sold it to a doll maker in Luray for a dollar before his family could get her in the ground. He knocked up a girl in Sperryville after he made sure to tell her he was from a town called Syria so her Daddy wouldn't be able to find him.

Red surprised everybody when he managed to talk a godly girl from Corbin Hollow named Sarah into marrying him. She had her work cut out for her with him, I'll tell you. The only thing Red liked to work at was sex. He knocked Sarah up five times in as many years. Rumor had it after baby number five she locked him out of her kitty except for his birthday and Christmas. I can't imagine Red going without so, if it was true, I guess he had his way with sheep at night.

When I found them outside at the shucking party, Torch and Red were fighting for a turn to prove who was man enough to muscle what looked to be a half-ton rock off the ground. Torch pushed his body into the rock and moaned with his eyes squeezed shut. He looked like a blind chipmunk trying to screw a pumpkin and I told him so. Torch said if he was screwing he'd pick a girl not a pumpkin and he'd be good at it. He offered me a chance to verify his skills first hand, but I told him to take a flying leap.

Red offered me a cigarette, which I was fool enough to take. He handed me a book of nudie matches with three naked girls painted on the paper folder and across each comb inside, so that every match you tore out had tits or ass on it. Then he said, "Go 'head, grab yourself a piece of ass, Bee," which cracked Torch up.

I pulled loose a match with a big pair of knockers on it and held it out to Red. "Aww Red, don't you want this one? From what I've heard, these are the only hooters you'll get your hands on 'til Christmas."

Torch and Peter both yucked it up at my joke. Red did not. His face turned ruddy as his hair. He changed the subject quick as he could. "Peter," he said, "play us that song Bee's partial to. That ought to shut her up for a while."

Peter loved to sing, so it didn't take any more encouragement then Red asking. Peter had a voice that would shake the ground much as any storm's thunder. I didn't mind since he was singing my favorite love story. I know you want to correct me and tell me to call it a song not a story, but if you let it sit with you a minute you've got to agree songs are just stories set to music, like the one Peter sang about two lovers who died young and got buried toe to toe:

They buried Willie in the old churchyard,

And Barbara there anigh him,

And out of his grave grew a red, red rose,

And out of hers, a briar.

They grew and grew in the old churchyard,

Till they could grow no higher,

They lapped and tied in a true love's knot.

The rose ran round the briar.

When Peter finished it was quiet for a while, then the real talk started. I'll try my best to lay it out for you here, since the men were full of news about the Hollow getting turned into a park so that city folks could come weekends and crunch pine needles under their feet.

Red, whose daddy Wilbur was so long in the tooth even his skin was gray, said Wilbur'd been threatening to die ever since they got the letter that said to clear out. Red told his daddy not to worry, because the government was going to buy everybody's land and they were giving away farms down mountain to boot. I wasn't sure that was much comfort to Old Wilbur. He'd been walking cockeyed up our rocky hillsides for so long I suspected his body might not work right on level land.

Torch accused Red of being fool enough to buy a bottle of sugar water from a traveling salesman if the swindler said it would fix his tongue. Red ate a lye soap cake when he was a boy and it burned the inside of his mouth so badly his r's sounded more like w's. Torch's remark wasn't a kindly one, but meanness was the way Torch and Red related. Anyway, everybody was fit to be tied about the government's letter, so folks were more hard edges than usual. When Torch talked about being forced to leave, his words came out in a soft growl like a hurt animal warning you off. Made me want to touch him to see if he'd take a bite out of me.

Torch went on to calculate that if the government handed out free farms to all five hundred of us left across four hollows it would go bankrupt. Torch got all kinds of smart ideas from the folks who stopped in at his daddy's general store. It had a gas pump out front so they came from all over. He picked up a more refined way of talking there too, so sometimes he sounded more like an out-of-towner than a mountain boy. I was sure the store was where he picked up his bankruptcy notion.

Torch's remark started a heated debate about whether he was calling Red a liar. At the end of it, Torch called Red a backwoods brain and said we'd all be lucky to get pennies on the dollar for what our land was worth. Apparently, he'd heard Arnie Ross, from over in Corbin Hollow, talking down at the store. Arnie didn't file papers at the county courthouse when he bought his land, so the government was calling him a squatter and saying they wouldn't pay him a red cent. I wouldn't have believed it if it wasn't happening to Mama and me. Torch said they weren't giving away farms either. "We've got to pay. My question is, if we don't get a fair price for our land here, how in the sam hill do they think we can afford to buy government land?"

Right about that time Red's face started to look like a hog's on killing day (I don't know how those pigs know it, but they do. You look into their nervous little eyes and tell me otherwise). I remember exactly what he said, because he sort of croaked it. "You saying we ain't gonna get nothing?"

Peter didn't like to see anybody in a tough spot (you'd never see hide nor hair of him come slaughter time), so he spoke up. He was rawboned, with a heart so big it was a miracle his thin frame could hold it. He told Red not to worry, that the government just wanted us out while they laid the park roads. "They gonna let us come on back," he said. "It's just for a spell, Red. Just for a spell." All three men went mute after that. The festive mood they'd shared before had gone right out of them.

Peter's family landed in the Hollow smack in the middle of the 1800s and built a two-story frame house three windows wide, with four rooms and a stone chimney -- pretty fancy for those parts. They farmed the land and made an honest living, if not always a good-sized one. Every one of Peter's kin who kicked the bucket since then was buried on that land. When Ruth's mama and daddy passed after she married Peter, she buried them there too.

There were others who'd gone down the mountain. Indians lived there and left. They killed deer with stone-tipped arrows and stretched their hides across boulders to dry in the sun. There were Negroes there once too, slaves to the families that could afford them. As soon as Mr. Lincoln won the war between the states, they went away. Seems like all those folks were going toward something. Food. Freedom. There wasn't anything waiting for us. Our houses and our dead were on Ragged Mountain.

| WHEN TORCH'S MAMA BURNED |

Mama and I went down to MacArthur's Store the day after the shucking. I was nervous to go since I could tell she was in a mood. She'd been slamming and banging around the house all morning grumbling about how a refined woman like her didn't belong in such a hell hole.

You remember me telling you Mama was a city girl from Richmond? The state hired her straight out of teachers' college to come learn the poor Hollow kids how to read and write and add numbers. Twenty-year-old Mama (who wasn't Mama then, just Ada Wilkins) showed up with some textbooks, a year's worth of pencils and paper, four dresses with matching pinafores she made herself from McCall's patterns and plans to go back home at the end of her contract and find a city man for a husband. I guess she didn't count on meeting my Daddy. He was a handsome devil then and a Livingston to boot -- the whole Hollow named for his family. He wooed Mama in a hurry. They got married a year and a half after they first laid eyes on each other. I gather Mama regretted it later.

The way Daddy told it to me, she was pretty in a plain, pleasant way. A person's eyes could pass over her without stopping to admire any one particular feature, but end with a sense of general good looks. It was her impeccable grooming that got his curiosity up. He said she never had a hair out of place or a torn hemline. Everything about her appearance was carefully attended to. Then he found out she could carry on a good conversation about something other than apple harvesting and he was hooked.

She griped the whole way down the mountain to the store. She'd been in a beastly mood since Rowler's visit. She said we couldn't afford to pay outright for one of those resettlement houses. The folks handing out the loans turned her down since nobody was giving her a paycheck, and our milk cow Daisy didn't exactly count as what they called collateral.

When Mama was irritated, every word that came out of her mouth was hard and sharp and pointed right at me. Sometimes when she was done talking I'd think I should check myself for welts. I did a poor job sweeping the house that morning and she called me a pig. She spit it at me like she would a sour cherry pit. A sharp ache bloomed behind my ribs the same as if she'd punched me. She said she was sorry for it later. She was under a strain, she said, because of the trouble I was giving her over Rowler. A tougher girl would have told her where she could stick her strain.

At least it was no surprise. She'd always called me names and always had a reason handy why it was my fault. It wouldn't surprise me to learn that once upon a time she stood over baby me in the cradle and called me a hellcat when I cried for milk. No matter what she called me, I didn't say boo when she apologized. It was nice to be in her good graces, even if it was only for a little while. I didn't have it in me to spoil it.

The sight of MacArthur's lifted my spirits. The mountain had been sad and gray with fog for a week. In the midst of it, the store glowed like a prize -- a colored Easter egg in the tall grass. A few men in rockers on the front porch mixed their meaty pipe smoke with the thin mountain air. Inside, the shelves and counters were stocked with manna from heaven. Golden, gleaming jars of syrupy honey next to the cash box. Jewel-colored candies piled sweetly in clear bins. Bolts of flowery calico fabric lined up in carefully-plotted garden rows.

Torch threw me a look when we walked in. When I got close enough, he nodded in Mama's direction and whispered to me, "Good thing you don't take after her. That woman's mad as a March hare." Then he winked. His daddy was the MacArthur of MacArthur's Store, so Torch worked behind the counter most days. He could tell when Mama had flattened me and he always thought of something clever to say to pick my spirits up. Even though she'd known him since he was born, Mama didn't have so much as a hello for Torch. She read her list off to him like she would a stranger.

Torch never gave Mama a reason not to like him, except he had trouble packing up our groceries on account of his ruined hands. Once he let go of a bag of coffee that busted open on the floor and peppered our feet with its black-brown grains. Just when I was sure I'd cleared the grounds from inside my shoes, I'd feel their grit scour my toes. By the time we got home, our stockings were stained brown as our old bay mare. It was such a terrible shame to waste good coffee, especially when most folks had taken to stewing up chicory root since the real thing got to thirty cents a pound. I sure wish I'd swept those coffee grounds from underfoot right into a pot and brewed them, even if it would have given Mama apoplexy. Anyway, ever since the occasion of the spilled coffee, Mama got cross with Torch and didn't try to hide it.

You're probably wondering what in God's name happened to Torch's hands. He burned them up trying to save his mama from blackening like toast left on the stove too long.

Torch was twelve when his daddy set him and his two older brothers to work clearing a spot for a smokehouse. Hiram, that's Torch's daddy, figured he could grow his profits if he smoked his own meat instead of paying somebody else to do it. Hiram had plans to plant too, so he wanted a good five acres cleared. The boys took the south side closest to the store and their daddy went to the north edge by the woods. They'd cleared the big trees the week before and they were on to the fun part: putting torches to the underbrush. Their Daddy told them to set two or three little fires at a time, then wait for those to peter out before lighting more. Torch's brothers were each just short of twenty years, so they figured they knew as much as their Daddy about how to handle brush fires. As soon as he was a few hundred paces away, they lit up more than they should've.

Torch's mama came out with a pitcher of water for her boys mid-morning. I guess she couldn't see her way through the curtains of smoke because she wandered right into a circle made by two nasty, whopper fires that linked their blazing hands behind her and wouldn't let her out. She hollered for one of her grown sons to come save her, but those twin fires joined to become Job's Leviathan set alight. The two boys who were of an age to beat it shrank from its breath. It was Torch who ran to save his mama from the beast. And when the flames made quick work of his soft, boy flesh, he kept on until he could lay hands on his mama and drag her back from hell.

Torch's mama died the next day. He spent the next few weeks crying over her, hacking up jagged bits of charcoal and seeping blood and water from the raw meat left on the parts of him the fire got. Folks liked to say God spared his face. Why the hell God would take the mama that boy loved more than puppies and jawbreakers put together but save his damned face was beyond me. What good did handsome do when there was a field to be plowed or bushels of apples that needed drying? But folks did like to admire him.

He had a gypsy's features, dusky and secretive. The skin on his face was perfect as a doll's except for a tiny burned patch on his jaw. His eyes were dark as they could be and still be called brown, with lashes crowded enough to give off an awning's shade. He'd have been almost too pretty if he ever smiled. He only showed me his teeth once after his mama died. It was the time he dared me to throw rocks at a hornets' nest. When they swarmed me, I tore my shirt off and whipped it at them all the way down to Brokenback Run, where I dunked my whole self in the water. Torch laughed until he couldn't catch breath.

Soon as his mama was buried, folks started calling him Torch instead of his given name, Daniel. He was a hero, even to the hoary veterans who left arms and legs at field hospitals during the War Between the States. I suppose the nickname was our way of letting him know how proud we were of him without saying it. Torch didn't have much use for his hero status. After the fire, he avoided people. If he hadn't been made to work the counter at the store on account of his brothers both leaving for jobs in Sperryville, he'd only have seen me and his daddy.

Speaking of those good-for-nothing brothers, he had them to thank for his bad hands. Doc Waters warned those boys not to let Torch's fingers cozy up together for too long or they'd stay that way. Hiram wasn't much help since he couldn't even look at Torch until after those burns stopped their weeping. But every touch from his brothers drew a scream from Torch, out of pain or anger at them for failing his mama or both -- until they couldn't stand it any more and just let him be. In the end, his left hand was just some nubs that looked like they'd been sewn together. His right hand was better. Just his middle two fingers were joined and the rest were free to move on their own.

More than a few women made eyes at Hiram once his wife's body (or what was left of it after her skirt burned right off and took most of the meat on her legs with it) was in the ground. He took on Heathcliff's mournful aspect after his wife passed, and I suppose each of them thought it was their womanly duty to buck him up. He paid them no mind. Mama said his temperance was to be admired. She said more to him in the fifteen minutes we were in the store than she did to me in a week. The two of them talked about whatever was in the newspaper mostly. Sometimes she'd ask him what was selling best or give him tips, like which brand of lye she thought was better than the others.

That day Hiram came out from the back to chat with Mama while

Torch boxed up our supplies. Torch carried our box out onto the store's porch steps. He motioned for me to sit close to him on the top step, like he was going to tell me a secret, then pulled a small jar of honey out of the box and handed it to me. I caught sight of that sweet amber liquid and sucked in a quick gulp of air that sent me into a coughing fit. "It's just honey," Torch said. "It's not like I proposed." Did I mention he could be insufferable? I told him the devil would get ahold of him one day for being too big for his britches. Of course I knew it was just honey, but it was glorious on top of a biscuit. Anyway, I also knew Mama hadn't ordered it. Lately, the least little thing set her off, so I figured it was best not to give her an excuse to lose her temper with me again.

I told Torch to put it back before he got me whipped for taking something we didn't pay for. Torch said I wouldn't give it back if my camera-toting friend gave it to me (he knew about Miles because I told him, and he ran the post office at the store where Miles sent his letters for me). I named a few Hollow girls who would have been over the moon if he gave them a river rock, much less a jar of honey. I told him he ought to save his presents for a girl who'd let him get past her drawers.

Torch stared at the jar of honey in my hands and asked me about what must have been troubling him since I toured Miles around the Hollow: "You gonna run off with that photographer?"

Here's where I feel like I ought to explain me and Torch. We came up like brother and sister but once I sprouted hooters, he got it in his head he wanted things to change. He tried everything he could think of to woo me. The honey was just about the end of it. He gave up while he could still lay claim to his pride. He was a proud man, my Torch. Even then he was a man. I was so short on sense I could only see the boy I knew too well. I was sure I was meant to fall in love with someone exciting and mysterious. Torch was so familiar I could guess what he was going to say before the words came out of his mouth. I was sure I couldn't kiss him and then go back to beating him in pissing contests (I'll bet you didn't know us girls can shoot it just as far as any men). On the hottest summer days, we laid in Brokenback Run's cool water and didn't say a word for hours, just listened to the water talk. All I could think back then was if we started up, we'd have had to take off our wet clothes and roll around instead of laying quiet. I was sure that would ruin things.

"I guess I would have run off with him already if I wanted to," I said. "You gonna elope with Janie Johnson and leave me here alone?"

"I might if you don't wise up," Torch said and smiled. Then his mouth flattened into a straight line. "What's got you all stirred up over him?"

"He's got stories to tell, and I can write him about mine since he doesn't know them all already," I said. Then I joked, "Plus, he's good in the sack." And I punched Torch in the arm. Torch grunted and got up to go back into the store. "You're just pissy because you haven't bagged Janie Johnson yet," I hollered after him.

Mama walked out of the store a second later, and there I was holding that damned jar of honey. Lucky for me she was all flushed from her chat with handsome Hiram. I slipped it into my jacket pocket before she noticed.

Your love is sweet as honey to me, my own Amelia. No child in the world is more doted on than you. I made an awful lot of mistakes in my time. Not giving Torch a chance sooner was one. You'll read about more of them soon enough. I imagine I'll look different to you by the time you finish reading this story. Maybe it'll help you steer clear of some mistakes of your own.

| WHEN THE MCCONVILLE'S BABY GOT STOLEN |

Mama and I went to the McConville's twice a month. They were one of the most down-on-their-luck families in the Hollow. They lived on land Franklin McConville laid claim to for free because no one else wanted it. Most of it was so steep and rocky it wasn't worth the trouble to clear out the pines. They had a one-room cabin (I've seen bigger spring houses) that had to fit Franklin, his wife Jenny, three boys and their nine-year-old girl Geraldine. All four kids slept in the loft. They packed it half full of corn husks to keep the cold out, but Geraldine told me some winter months the weather drifted in through the cracks and they woke up with snow for blankets.

The downstairs had almost no furniture, just the marriage bed, a table too small to fit the whole family and a few chairs Franklin rigged from rough-hewn wood he found in a trash heap behind a lumber mill. Jenny kept the inside clean as Jesus' conscience. She papered the walls with Sears and Roebuck catalogs for decoration. There were pages of rifles, shoes, wood stoves and little boys in bright blue sailor suits. My favorites were the ones from the Sears Modern Homes Catalog. There was a two-story house called the Amsterdam that was pictured in black and white. I saw it in color. Red and yellow tulips in window boxes, blue clapboard siding and a rooftop the orange of a dying oak leaf. I'd learned enough from Mama's geography lessons to know Amsterdam was a city but in spite of its name, I thought that house belonged on a country lane flanked by a round, red windmill.

One of the pages on the McConvilles' wall advertised a Simplex portable outhouse, four-feet square, for forty-one dollars. It had been circled by a finger dipped in black soot, probably Jenny's. None of the McConvilles had ever felt the weight of more than a dollar in his palm, so they weren't likely to order the Simplex or any other fancy outhouse anytime soon. Both Franklin and his wife Jenny worked at a resort near the Hollow called Mountaintop, when its owner, a real goddamned bastard named Buddy Collins, could afford to pay them. Even then, Buddy was known to pay his people in dishes or forgotten, fake ruby brooches found in guests' rooms. Franklin did odd jobs when he was sober. Jenny washed the resort laundry in fat tubs that lolled in her front yard, waiting to be fed lumpy mouthfuls of dirty bedclothes.

About a year before the trouble with the government started, Jenny asked Mama and me to teach her and Geraldine how to read and write. The rest of the family never turned a page. Franklin said reading the newspaper wouldn't put food on his table so he wasn't interested. He convinced their three boys he was right. The truth was Franklin hadn't been interested in anything but white mule since the day they took his youngest boy away.

It happened when Buddy paraded some government folks through the Hollow to convince them to turn us into a park. One of them was a lady social worker who took an interest in the littlest McConville, George. The boy had just seen his third birthday, but he wasn't any bigger than if he'd been a whole year younger. His belly was round as a pregnant woman's and his legs were so badly bowed you could ride a wagon through them. The social worker said he had rickets. She told Jenny they'd take him to a hospital in town for a few weeks and see to it that he got the care he needed. When Jenny saw him again, the lady said, George would be a happy, healthy boy.

Jenny loved that boy as much as any of her kids, which I can tell you was a hell of a lot. She cried when they took George. Franklin teased her for it. He said George would be back before they knew it. Jenny walked the five miles down to MacArthur's every day, looking for letters from the social worker with news about her boy. And every day, she dictated a letter to Torch. "I been waiting for word about my boy," Torch would write her words in his hand and sneak in a few corrections to make her sound less hillbilly. "You reckon he'll be home soon? My arms ain't been feeling right without him to tote around." This went on for months. Finally, word came. George was well, but he wouldn't be coming home. It was for the best, the social worker wrote. After all, the McConvilles couldn't really afford the children they had. George would be better off with a family in town. He'd already been adopted, she said. There was no getting him back. Jenny took to her bed for weeks. Franklin said there was nothing left for him to do except drink until it killed him.

Torch saw little George once in Luray, outside a hardware store. He was chubby and rosy-cheeked. He sat on top of one of those metal ponies kids can ride for a nickel. His new mama was watching him, smiling and holding his coat -- a pretty blue one with brass buttons.

It was after she got over the shock of it that Jenny came to ask Mama and me to tutor her and Geraldine. She said if somebody in her family had been educated, they wouldn't have taken George. She damn sure well wasn't going to let it happen again. Maybe she thought she could figure out a way to bring him home.

Jenny was still stuck on the Dick and Jane readers, even after months of Mama trying to teach her. I don't know how a grown woman could stand the repetition in those books. "Oh, see. Oh, see Jane. Funny, funny Jane." Seems to me like whoever wrote those stories wasn't right in the head. A person could go crazy from reading them time and time again. Poor Jenny. She tripped and stumbled over the silly words.

Geraldine was a good reader. The Velveteen Rabbit was her favorite book. Mama made Geraldine and me read poetry aloud instead. She said the verse's meter would help Geraldine learn to talk like a civilized young lady instead of a mountain girl. Geraldine liked poems about nature, and I found a few in Mama's books. Our favorite was one about a snake, written by a man called D.H. Lawrence. We especially liked it because Mama said the writer was no better than a pornographer and forbid our reading of it. When I asked her why she bought a book she considered wicked, she said Daddy gave it to her because he didn't know any better.

Once I knew Daddy's hands had touched the book, I studied it carefully and saw that the page with the snake poem had been dog-eared. I'm sure it was Daddy who did it. Mama didn't let me bring the book to the McConvilles', so I copied down the words on a piece of scrap paper I kept hidden in a King James Bible. Geraldine and I memorized the whole poem. We whispered it to each other when Mama and Jenny were paying us no mind. It would have tickled Daddy to know it.

I'll copy a few of the words down here. Maybe you could read them aloud too. I guess that will be as close as you'll come to speaking with your Grandaddy.

And I wished he would come back, my snake.

For he seemed to me again like a king,

Like a king in exile, uncrowned in the underworld,

Now due to be crowned again.

And so, I missed my chance with one of the lords

Of life.

After we finished the week's lessons, Jenny insisted on serving us supper. It was important to her to feed us in return for our teaching. I always felt bad about it since I knew her family would leave the table hungry the next day to make up for what we ate. That night Jenny served up corn pone with fried fat back, which might as well have been gold coins for all it was worth to them. Franklin's eyes followed our forks every time they carried the food to our mouths. I made it up to him after supper, though. I managed to carry a mason jar full of Daddy's last batch of white mule in my book sack along with Torch's honey with Mama none the wiser. After supper, I excused myself to go to the necessary house (which for the McConvilles was a lean-to that sure enough leaned to and fro when the wind blew). Then I went to the spring house instead and left the whiskey and Torch's honey jar.

Before we left, Mama read to the family from the Bible -- everyone except Franklin who had gone somewhere to get drunk. The McConvilles didn't have a proper fireplace, so we all sat on the floor in front of the rusted metal barrel they used as hearth and cookstove. By the time Mama got to the part where they shut Daniel in the lions' den, Geraldine was curled up with her head in her mama's lap. Jenny stroked Geraldine's hair absentmindedly, natural, like Geraldine was part of her.

On the way home, Mama asked me did I want to end up like the McConvilles. She said if I married a mountain man that might be my lot. "That state man could take you away from here," she said. "And me too, for that matter. A man like that would provide for his mother-in-law. He could certainly afford to. People would be impressed you made such a good catch."

I told her I didn't care about impressing anybody. "Rowler's not going to save us, Mama," I said. "I don't trust him and I don't want anything to do with him."

She went on and on about his being middle class, like that put him right up there with the Queen of Sheba. It was beyond me how she could be so taken with the size of a man's wallet she couldn't see him for the rat he was.

| THE FIRST EVICTION |

It wasn't long before that state man Rowler came back. This time, he didn't even bother to scrape the mud off his boots before he stepped into the house. As if that wasn't insult enough, he helped himself to a seat at our table, then told Mama he wanted coffee. "I take mine with milk, two sugars," he said, pretty as you please. I waited for Mama to tell him what he could do with himself, but all she did was put the coffee on. I watched him write an inventory of our property in a notebook: one milk cow, one sow with piglets, one mule, one bay mare, one cracked leather saddle, horse collar, harness, shovel plow, bear trap, churn. You get the idea. I realized when I saw the list leak from his pencil onto the page that he must have poked around in the barn before he came up to the house to announce himself.

He told Mama he was stopping at every house in the Hollow to let folks know what would happen to anybody who didn't agree to clear out on their own steam. He said we'd be arrested -- dragged off our land. That's when he showed us a newspaper clipping about Eliza and Henry Taylor from over in Corbin Hollow. He took care to smooth the creases after he pulled it from his shirt pocket. "Damn shame what she forced us to do," he said. He clucked the way people do when they're pretending to be sorry about something. The article was from the Richmond paper the day before. The headline read, "Squatters Refuse to Vacate State Land."

I almost didn't recognize Eliza. Daddy and Eliza's husband Henry were friends from boyhood. Daddy used to take me with him to call on them, so I knew what Eliza looked like. Her face in the picture was screwed up in a way that scared me to look at. I checked for the roundness of her pregnant middle to be sure it was her (the last time I saw her at MacArthur's, she was six months along). In the picture, two men I didn't recognize had lifted her clear off the ground so they could cart her away.

Her belly hung down between them, big, like she'd swallowed the moon. The story said Henry and Eliza were on land that belonged to Virginia, but I could see their house in the background clear as day. Henry was kneeling in the little square patch where Eliza's daffodils popped their yellow heads up every year. His hands were behind his back. Rowler told us he'd handcuffed Henry for being unruly.

Rowler said we'd be carted off the same as the Taylors if we made trouble. He said we were lucky he was giving us five months to get out. If we played our cards right, we could get one of the houses the government built for people from the hollows for free. "Of course, if you don't agree to my earlier offer," he said, "you could always pay for the house yourselves." He looked in Mama's direction. "I don't imagine you've got much of a nest egg, though, have you? I took the liberty of looking around the place, and I don't see anything that would qualify as collateral for a loan. Of course, I'm no banker. You're welcome to try your luck with one. I'll wait. Not forever though."

I started to tell him to stick it where the sun don't shine but before I could say more than "Now you listen here," Mama grabbed my arm and squeezed it too hard. That's what she used to do when she wanted me to hush up before I embarrassed her.

Rowler reached into the wooden bowl we kept on the sideboard, plucked an apple and bit into it while he made eyes at me. Mama asked me to walk him to the front gate. She had her jaw set in a way that let me know I'd better not say no.

Rowler's talk was harmless, about the weather or some such thing, until we got to the end of the yard where Mama couldn't hear us anymore. He pulled a pack of Lucky Strikes from his shirt pocket and held them out to me. I could have used a smoke right about then, but I wouldn't have taken a bucket of water from that man if I was on fire. He gave his shoulders a suit-yourself shrug. He looked me over while he took a drag, then leaned in close and whispered, "I'll have you one way or another." I was struck dumb. I may not have come across too many men of Rowler's sort, but I knew a threat when I heard one. It wasn't until he stepped away and daylight hit me that I realized he'd been looming over me, blocking the sun.

Mama was waiting on the porch. "What'd he say?"

"He said he'd have me one way or another," I said. "I think he was trying to scare me."

"Ada Anabelle Livingston. You may not like the man," she said, "but that's no excuse for telling stories. Mr. Rowler is a government man. Middle class. Men like him don't say things like that."

"Why don't you believe me? You heard him say it would take time with me to bring out his generous nature. Do you really think he wants to play goddamn checkers?"

"That's enough. If you can't act like you've been raised better than an animal, you can sleep with them in the barn." She went inside. A minute later she was back with a quilt she threw in my face.

I've heard people say God picks your parents. He may strike me down with a lightning bolt for saying it, but he made a mistake putting me and Mama together.

There was another picture in that newspaper article that bothered me almost as much as the first. It was one I saw Miles take of the old Alexander cabin on the west side of the Hollow. I took him there the first day we spent together when he said he wanted to see the most rundown homesteads. The caption under it said, "Most mountain hillbillies live in shacks no better than animal dens."

I was awake all night that night, wondering whether Miles knew they would use his photos to make us out to be beasts. How could he? My heart told me he was too good a man to try to hurt us with his pictures. I told myself it was the newspaper's fault. Of course his bosses at the Resettlement Administration would have sent more than one photo. Maybe they included a picture of Ruth's beautiful new barn or the freshly-painted metal roof on MacArthur's Store. The trouble was I couldn't quite convince myself it was the newspaper that got it wrong. I asked Miles about it in my next letter. His answer back threw me.

Miles went back to Washington between us and Alabama. His boss liked his pictures -- told him they were exactly what Uncle Sam needed to paint us as hillbillies. Turns out the government was after the public to give them the go ahead to move us to a better place where we could clean ourselves with running water and learn not to marry our close cousins. Miles told him the truth about us was nothing like what folks in Washington were saying. The boss man laughed and said Miles was looking at us through rosy lenses on account of he'd had a few good rolls in the hay while he was here. This got Miles' hackles up. He wrote me line after line about how the boss man had no right to talk about me or any of us Hollow folks that way. But he never did a thing about it. I wouldn't call him lilly-livered. He just didn't have it in him to fight for us.

Before you get to wondering why I didn't give him the heave ho right then and there, you've got to understand Miles had an artist's constitution. He wasn't hardy like mountain folks. One time while he was up mountain, he tried to take a photo of Ruth killing a chicken. He swooned like a girl soon as the hatchet divorced that chicken from its head. Miles was a gentle soul. I knew from the start he wasn't the kind of man you'd bet on in a slugfest. That didn't matter a hill of beans to me. I didn't expect I'd need that kind of man around.

| SNEAKING OFF |

I was still hot to trot for Miles even after that business about the picture in the paper. I had a weakness for men, it was true. I heard women complain about men being unruly and not bathing often enough to wash away the stench of hard work. I always liked men all the more for their rough edges. I especially liked the way the scratch of a man's bristles on my cheek could make me forget what I was feeling before and only feel him. With Miles, I got a man's attention plus a treasure trove of stories about his travels. The problem was now that he was gone, he was only words on paper. I took to reading books to distract me from missing the feel of him. With a book as my companion, I was faithful to Miles as a starved dog to a master with a fat goose slung over one shoulder.

I was up to my neck in chores or Mama's schoolwork during daylight hours, so I had to get my books in when it was dark or close to it. Mostly that was at night cozied up to a lantern in the barn. But Sundays, when Mama would read the Bible to herself first thing, I could sneak off to the cornfield and hide between the whispering rows with a book. I only had to wait until night's black turned blue for there to be enough light to read by.

Truthfully, I can't remember a time when I didn't sneak off to read every chance I got. Seems like I came out of the womb holding a copy of *Alice's Adventures in Wonderland*. Daddy sent away to the Book League of America and got me a membership for my thirteenth birthday. It was like the Book of the Month Club, where they send you something new to read every four weeks, except I got two books: the best new book and one of the great classics, just like their ad said.

The best book I ever read came on my third month of Book League deliveries. It was written by a man named Billy Faulkner. That Faulkner had a cleverness like none I've seen. The way he wrote I felt like I was reading people's minds, like their wet brains had been pulled from their cracked-open skulls and laid out on the pages. He even spoke for a dead woman and made me believe it was really her talking.

Mama said we couldn't afford the twenty-one dollars it would cost for the next year's membership. I couldn't seem to go a day without feeling the weight of a book in my palms, so I had plans to read my old books over again once the new ones stopped coming. Then there was Mama's book of Greek myths. A favorite of mine. It had a picture of a flying horse called Pegasus inside. Zeus turned him into stars and put him in the sky. He flew over the mountain and he flies over you still, my darling Amelia. Look up at night and you'll see him in the stars, right here in the city sky.

| WHEN THE SNAKES KILLED DADDY |

There was so much talk about leaving, it struck me that I ought to try to earn some money for when the government made us head out. Kids in the hollows sold baskets and berries up at Mountaintop so I decided to give it a try, against my better judgement. Mountaintop was a retreat just west of us where people came to get away from the city noise. There were twelve cabins, six each on either side of an open field they used for putting on shows and teaching people how to ride horses. The main house was all stones stacked two stories high. Ruth liked to remind people that her daddy did the stone work. She should have been proud. That house looked like a castle on a Scottish moor.

Daddy never let me go to Mountaintop alone while he was alive and he never would have let me beg, which is what he said it was to get paid for berries anybody could pick themselves. I usually avoided Mountaintop. Buddy Collins had come down from Washington to build the place. It was his fault Daddy died. I'll try to tell you about how it happened, but I've got to work up to it.

The guests had money to spare. Some of the kids sold more berries than others. I studied how they did it. It required some dramatics.

First step was to make a dress out of a few burlap sacks. I left the ends frayed and tied it at the waist with some brown twine. Daddy kept an old bonnet his mama used to wear, so I tied that over my hair. I put old work shoes on my feet and patted myself all over with some loose dirt. I'd managed to weave five small baskets and pick enough blackberries to fill them -- no small task I can tell you -- so I carried them with me over Brokenback Run to Mountaintop.

Next step was to break their hearts with my wretchedness. It was like picking apples that have gone past ripe. They practically jump off the tree into your hands. I focused on the women mostly. Ruth used to say most women have an instinct to mother anybody younger than them. I tried to look small, talk small. When one lady, about half-way through life, asked me how much for some blackberries, I looked down and said whatever you think is fair ma'am. She said to just give her the whole lot (I had three baskets left) and paid me six dollars! My stomach felt a little funny afterward. I guess it was guilt over doing something Daddy told me not to. I rubbed the paper money between my fingers and that fixed me up.

I was almost to the trail back home when Buddy Collins came riding in on a chestnut gelding he called General. I swear that animal had mule in him, and I don't mean General. He was too fine a creature. Buddy was dressed like an Indian chief right out of a Western: leather shirt and pants, moccasins and a feathered headdress that teetered back and forth so wildly it looked as if his whole head might topple. His face was smeared with enough black and red war paint for a dozen Indian braves. The bow and arrow set slung across his chest was too small, probably a child's toy. Its string bunched up his leather shirt so that it hugged his pot belly. There was a glint of metal at his heels, tiny spurs an Indian never would have worn, no more humane for their small size. He pressed the sharp shine into General, then pulled back hard on the reins. General didn't know whether to go forward or backward, so he seesawed in place. His skin around the saddle pad started to foam white from the effort of it. When Buddy tipped his hat, the city folks cheered and cheered.

I admit I was mesmerized by the spectacle. I turned to leave too late. Buddy laid eyes on me, ran General past and jerked him to a halt between me and the trail head. We were a dozen yards from the guests, but he shouted loud enough for them to hear, "Well if it isn't Bee Livingston, as I live and breathe," like we were long lost friends. Buddy liked to pretend he was our great benefactor. Hollow folks saw it differently.

When the guests seemed satisfied that the great Buddy Collins was looking after me, they lost interest and circled around the berries. Buddy slid from General's back onto the ground by my side. Buddy was a good one hand shorter than me, if you measured him the way you would a jackass. A lifetime of sidestepping hard work had made him flabby. Half of his hair had jumped ship. His pinkish scalp glowed from beneath what was left, vulnerable in the afternoon sun.

He must have been in a crowing mood that night, because he spent a good long time telling me how it was him who got us picked to be a national park. Apparently he brought a state senator to Mountaintop, filled him full of good whiskey, then hiked him to the top of Ragged Mountain to see one of our sunsets. The senator was so taken with the place he convinced the Governor to come, then the Governor recruited a United States Senator and so on. They all fell for our mountain thanks to Buddy's game of political dominoes.

I told Buddy I wouldn't recommend bragging about it. He ignored me.

"You mountain people aren't so sure about it now," he said. "That's only natural." Even though Buddy had lived on the mountain for twenty years, he'd never mixed much with Hollow folk. He saw us as a few rungs down on the ladder. "I'm the sole visionary here," he kept on even though I hadn't asked. "It is quite a burden to be the only one capable of securing the future of these mountains. But I've managed to lasso a boon and bring it home to you people. You'll all see that in time."

"When will that be," I asked him, "after they take our land or later, when we're homeless on the side of the road?"

"It will all be evident in time, my dear."

"I guess you think you'll make a pretty penny once the park opens, being that your place is the only lodging anywhere in the mountains."

"We'll all benefit. Don't you see? Most of my profits go to mountain people, my hired hands. And the more I make, the more people I can employ."

I could see that the only person who was going to benefit from Buddy's scheme to get more guests into Mountaintop was Buddy. I wasn't in the mood for a prolonged debate on the matter, so I let it go. Buddy started in on me about firing up Daddy's old still. Daddy sometimes sold as many as twenty quarts a week at Mountaintop. Buddy said Red Monroe was hawking his whiskey up there but the guests were complaining about the quality.

He asked me how much I made selling baskets. When I told him, he laughed and said it was just a drop in the bucket compared with what I could make selling good whiskey. I knew how to work the still. Daddy taught me how to make decent whiskey by taking my time and using only the sweetest corn. Then Buddy said I'd be helping him out. I didn't want to help that man. Daddy was dead because of him.

After I said I'd think about it, Buddy dragged me back to the field between the cabins for the snake show. He said if I watched, I'd see that what happened to Daddy was an accident that couldn't be helped. Morbid curiosity made me stay. I wasn't there the day Daddy died. I only saw him later at the house, swollen bruises puffed around fang-shaped pockmarks.

A boy named Sam Nelson whose family lived above the creek came walking from the stone castle house carrying a bag of snakes that twitched like a man on the gallows. The canvas seized in fits, hopping and swaying, putting on a show for a bunch of gawkers. I had the urge to slice it open with a scything blade so I could hear the snakes' meaty bodies smack the ground.

I didn't see Buddy leave, but here he was back in a different costume. He was dressed like a dirt poor mountain man with a big wooden cross around his neck instead of the bow and arrow that was there before. Sam introduced him as a mountain pentecost who communed with snakes. First thing Buddy did was hold up a Bible and shout, "Behold, I give unto you power to tread on serpents and scorpions, and over all the power of the enemy and nothing shall by any means hurt you." Then he slipped a knotty old pine branch into the bag and came up with a timber rattler. It was slow. Too slow. It's scales were dull. It was so withered I could have wrapped the fingers of one hand around it and squeezed it to death without much protest. The city people didn't notice. A snake was a snake to them. They cheered like they had for General's discomfort. There were some gasps from the women. They were confounded.

There was no need to be. I'll tell you a secret that'll blow the mystery of snake charming wide open for you. Buddy kept the snakes in a bathtub with a section of tin roof on top, holes punched in it for air, cinderblocks and rocks on the corners. Once he bought the snakes from the Hollow men, he'd stick them in there and wouldn't feed them again. By the time he used them in the show, they were so sick with hunger they didn't have the inclination to bite anybody. Even if they did, they couldn't make enough venom to do much harm.

Buddy always hated to do the snake show, but even the guests who'd never been before knew enough to ask about it, so he used to pay Daddy to do it. The afternoon the snakes struck Daddy, Buddy was the one who picked them from the tub. The weasel picked the two velvet-tailed rattlers Daddy had delivered that morning, fresh from their den and pissed as hellfire. The way it was told to me, both snakes were wrapped around the stick when Daddy pulled it out of the bag, black heads big as saucers and yellow eyes. The first strike he took was to the face. The second was to the neck. He dropped the stick. They must have gotten him a time or two on the way down because I remember seeing swollen parts under his clothes when they carried him into the house.

Once they'd gotten Daddy into bed, Mama shut the door to the room they shared and told me to keep out. She said he needed his rest. A day and a night passed with the door closed and her guarding it like she was the sphinx and that room was Thebes. I told her I was going to milk Daisy, then I walked around back and sneaked in Daddy's window.

It hit me hard how breakable he looked. I was afraid to put my arms around him, so instead I held one of his hands between my two. I wasn't sure he knew it was me. I whispered in his ear that he'd get better soon. He smiled a little with the side of his face the snakes didn't get. He pulled his hand away, then rested it back on top of mine, holding my two little-girl hands in his one, big daddy hand. Then his breath stopped coming.

So now you know. I don't think I'll tell that story again. It takes the snuff out of me to remember Daddy that way.

At least I had seventeen years with my Daddy. I hate that you didn't have one minute with yours. That's not all true. He did hold you one time. I'll save that for the end of this story since right now I'm about full up of sadness and I expect I can't swallow any more.

| MAMA'S VIRGIL |

We drove all the way from our wild mountain to Richmond's paved smooth streets to ask Mama's people for money to save us from Rowler. Toward the end of the trip, Mother Nature was hot on our tailpipe. It was late in the year for a hurricane, but one roared into the city right behind us just the same. By the time we'd parked Daddy's beater truck in front of Mama's family home, all hell had broken loose. I'm convinced Mother Nature came for a visit and got pissy when she saw folks in Richmond had all but locked her out: buildings built tall enough to block the sun and the earth all paved over with only thin green stripes of grass peeking through here and there. I think she aimed to show those city folks she was still the boss. She walloped the city good with so much rain the James River outgrew its bed. Water claimed riverside cemeteries, blocks of city streets and the Fulton Gas Works on Williamsburg where Mama's stepdaddy Virgil ran the overnight shift.

Mama and Virgil got on about as good as a house cat and a feral dog. Mama's daddy died when she was a girl and Other Mama (that's what I called her instead of grandma) married Virgil the year Mama turned fifteen. Each saw the other as an interloper and that's where the trouble started. Virgil was probably the reason Mama left her own home to teach on our mountain. Maybe I should have thanked him for shooing Mama toward Daddy, since if he hadn't I never would have been born, except he was such a horse's ass I could hardly bring myself to say how do you do.

He put one of his clodhoppers down on a china doll Other Mama gave me one Christmas and smashed it all to pieces. He didn't do it on purpose, so I can't hold that part against him. But when I cried, he got real mad and yelled at me to shut up. I didn't like him much before and I sure didn't like him after.

I knew Mama planned to ask Virgil and Other Mama for money to get us out of the fix we were in with Rowler about to claim our place or me. What I couldn't figure out was why she thought nasty Virgil would give us one red cent. She said to let her worry about that so I did.

Other Mama was soft as Virgil was hard. I thought the world of her. At bedtime, she made up stories instead of reading them to me. She kept doing it, even after I'd grown up. She came up with some good ones, like the one about a world made all of candy with water fountains full of cherry Coca-Cola. Other Mama's hair went all white when she turned twenty six. She died it black as coal until after she turned sixty and set vanity aside. The way Virgil complained about the mismatched, messy way she dressed and the extra fat she carried around her middle, I guess he wished she and vanity were still bunkmates. Virgil was so vain it wouldn't have surprised me to learn he sneaked off to a beauty parlor to have his hair dyed (it was awfully dark for a man his age).

We spent a few nights in Richmond before Mama got around to what we came for. The storm distracted everybody at first. Soon as it let up, Virgil had to go to the gas works to take stock of the damage. He left for work around 9 that night, and didn't get home until noon the next day. We spent the morning playing Rook and helping Other Mama with the wash. She had an electric tub on the back porch that squeezed the clothes through two rollers to wring out the water. She and Virgil lived in the house my real grandaddy bought forty years before. It was in the part of the city where the streets fanned out on the map, a few blocks from Monument Street where the houses looked more like castles. The house was orderly in front, straight and square. In back, there was a Wisteria-covered porch and a small, sunny spot with room enough to grow a few rows of vegetables.

Virgil flopped down in one of the parlor chairs when he got home midday. I brought him a beer at Mama's urging. I'd never seen beer in a can before. It was made by a company called Krueger. I remember it cracked and spit when I opened it for him. Anyway, I figured Mama was going to make her move since she was having me butter Virgil up. We all sat down and listened to him tell about the mess at the gas works first.

The way Fulton was built, the boiler room was on the first floor. When the outer edges of the hurricane hit, the flood waters rose up high enough to knock out the boilers, then surrounded a reserve tank with twenty-four hours' worth of gas in it. Virgil made the call to shut off the city's gas to avoid blowing the whole place sky high. It sounded like a hellacious night and not the time to ask him for any favors. Mama did anyway.

"Virgil," she started, "I've been meaning to ask you something."

"What's that?" He took a long swig of his beer. The sound of him swallowing made me wish I had one of my own.

"I know you're a man who understands business so I won't waste your time. I'll get right to the point."

"Uh huh."

"The government is taking our land for a park. Anabelle and I have nowhere to go and no savings to speak of." I knew Mama was hoping he'd get the drift without her having to come right out and ask him for money. He probably knew it too, which is why all Virgil said was, "Uh huh" again. Mama straightened her skirt. She was looking down at it, working up the gumption to ask, when Other Mama stepped in.

"I think what she's saying, Virgil honey," she said, "is that they could use some help with money."

"Is that so?" Virgil's face stiffened the way it had when little-girl me cried over that broken doll. "What makes you think I have any money to give you? It's the goddamned Depression. Times are hard for everybody. Why should you get a handout?"

Mama answered quickly. She must have been saving the words on the tip of her tongue, waiting for the chance to spit them out. "You're living for free in the house my daddy bought and paid for. Maybe you could loan me a little bit of the money you've saved on house payments all these years."

Virgil's answer was to slam his fist down on the side table next to his chair. "You think your Daddy owned this place?" He laughed. "You stupid ninny. Your Daddy was a gambler who mortgaged this house three times over to pay his debts. After I married your mother, those banks came calling. I've worked my ass off for twenty years to pay what he owed. Your Daddy was a no good bum."

If it was possible to kill somebody dead with just a look, Mama would have murdered Virgil right then and there. Virgil flipped over the chair he'd been sitting in with one hand, then left the room without another word.

"He's had a hard night at work," Other Mama said. "You shouldn't talk to him like that. You know he wants to retire, but he has to keep on working because the gas company cut his pension. He's getting too old to work a young man's hours and not suffer for it."

"Why do you make excuses for him? He's a brut." Mama's diction was perfect as a movie star's. Some folks get sloppy when they get mad. Anger just served to make Mama more proper.

"Ada, don't get upset honey. Virgil's right. Without him, I would have lost the house to pay your Daddy's debts." Other Mama thought on it a minute, then she said, "Maybe there's another way. You and Anabelle could move in here."

"He'd never agree to that, and you won't push for it because you can't stand to make him mad."

"Well, the house is small. And he has to have quiet during the day so he can get his rest between work shifts." Other Mama thought on it a minute, then her voice got shrill with excitement. "I can give you the money!"

"You? Mother, you don't have a job. Where are you going to get the money?"

"My own daddy's life insurance. By the time the cancer got him, Virgil had already paid off your father's loans. So I socked some of it away in case Virgil died too and left me with nothing."

"Other Mama," I chimed in to avoid what I saw as impending heartbreak for her and Mama both. "If you have that money in a bank, it's gone by now. Have you talked to your banker? Is your bank even in business anymore?"

"Bank? Oh honey, you must think I'm a fool. I took that money out of the bank ages ago. It's stuffed in the cushion of that sofa you're sitting on."

She unzipped the sofa cushion which, come to think of it, had made a crinkling sound when I sat down on it. There must have been a hundred dollars in there. What a pretty sight it was! Mama said Other Mama had better not give it to us or Virgil would blow his top. Other Mama said Virgil didn't know about the money so he wouldn't miss it.

Mama carried the money up to our room tucked into her brassiere and the waistband of her skirt so Virgil wouldn't see it. She let out a big sigh after she stuffed it into our suitcase. Then she sat on top of the case like it needed hatching. She wasn't as over the moon as I expected her to be. I think she wanted to squeeze that money out of her stepdaddy, or at least get to fight with him some more over it. Mama wanted to rain her own storm down on Virgil.

I asked her if she was planning on buying a place in Richmond since it was home to her and she was never partial to the mountain. She said she'd already written to everyone she knew in the city asking about teaching jobs and there was nothing.

"This isn't enough to buy a place anyway," she said, patting the suitcase. "Not even one of those cheap resettlement houses the government is selling. I know you don't want to hear it, but we won't be set unless you convince Mr. Rowler to do us a good turn. Or did you think that photographer friend of yours was going to ride in on a white horse?"

It gave me a jolt to hear her mention Miles. Mama asked, didn't I think she knew about him. She said a few other things that made it clear she'd read at least some of his letters to me. I felt naked standing there, her knowing things I thought were secret. She almost had me believing he didn't care about me because he hadn't offered to help. "He's probably got a girl in every country town he's passed through, each of you dumb enough to think you're the only one."

I said that wasn't true. But when Mama asked me how I knew I didn't say. My good feeling about him wouldn't have been enough to satisfy her.

I never intended to live with Mama after we got kicked off our place. I didn't tell her because I didn't want to get her all worked up. Instead I wrote to Miles to ask if he could use a photographer's helper. Miles said the road was no place for me. Too many rough characters. I used my next few letters to try to convince him. It didn't work. So be it, I remember thinking. Wherever I ended up, it wouldn't be with Mama. She was my own Virgil. We'd never see eye to eye.

| DEADLY NIGHTSHADE TEA |

Mama put me to work on my lessons soon as we got back from Richmond. I spent half of one day without even a break to visit the necessary house. The Hollow school had closed once money ran out to pay for it, but I was still obliged to be her student. Our first day back it was history and arithmetic, the two most tedious subjects ever invented. Every time my eyes wandered away from her over to the window, Mama whacked my fingers with a ruler. About an hour in I prayed for the learning to be over.

She'd been riding me hard, like I was some green pony she was trying to break. Seemed like she'd have picked a china doll over a real live girl for a daughter. I reckon she'd have found me much more agreeable if I had a painted-on mouth that didn't open. She could have dressed me and posed me like she wanted. Spoken for me in a sweet, ladylike voice. Sent me off with Rowler, too.

Soon as Mama left me to my own devices I dropped the books and headed to Ruth's. From time to time, Ruth gave me lessons in something useful: healing. She was our very own medicine woman. She liked to say she was going to leave me the business. The truth was that most of the people she helped couldn't afford to pay her, not in cash anyway.

We spent that night on prince's pine and deadly nightshade. Prince's pine plants have coy little flowers that bend their heads to hide their faces. We left the blossoms alone. All we needed were the leaves for a tea to cure dropsy. We made a batch for Mrs. Bauer. She was near about eighty and had a leg so swollen it looked like pink pig's meat. Next time Ruth said we'd hold a little prince's pine back. She could make an awfully good root beer with it.

Ruth had been waiting on the deadly nightshade until I got some experience under my belt. It's so poisonous it can kill a grown man who eats just one of its berries. But if you boil it in water, it can cure a whole host of ills. The trick is to strain the tea three times. Then you can be sure that wicked sister didn't sneak any bits of her past you.

Deadly nightshade tea was Ruth's specialty. It's best used for mumps. It's too bad Ruth wasn't making her tea back when her husband Peter swelled up. They were just kids then, not married yet and Ruth too young to know how to heal. She told me the mumps went down on Peter. Grew his balls to the size of Stayman apples. His manhood (I'll call it that in case when you read this you're still young enough to get embarrassed by words like pecker or jigglestick) shot blood like a turkey's neck on the chopping block. Ruth said Peter's manhood still worked for all the important stuff, but the mumps might have been why he'd never given her a child.

Ruth had been helping Hollow women bring babies into the world since she was a young girl herself. Peter was sure that, since she hadn't managed to become a mother yet, Ruth never would hold a baby of her own. Ruth still believed in miracles.

You'd need all your fingers and toes and all of somebody else's to count how many babies Ruth delivered in her time. She had some close calls, like when the Haner's second baby came out ass first and got stuck in her mama's front garden, if you get my drift. Ruth grabbed a hold of that slimy-as-a-wet-toad baby and jerked her up, down and sideways until she slid out and her Mama hollered "Praise Jesus" so loud they heard her in heaven. Of course, there were some babies Ruth couldn't save -- the ones that left this world before they set a tiny foot in it. When a baby dies in the womb, it's got to come out just the same. Ruth gave those women ground black snakeroot and pennyroyal leaves to hurry things along.

She told them to save what came out in a mason jar and bring it back to her, so she could make sure everything left that was supposed to. No one but me and Ruth knew it, but she kept those motherless babies floating in formaldehyde-filled mason jars on wooden shelves in her back pantry. I found them when I brought Ruth the I-appreciate-you apple pie Mama made for her after Ruth helped her beat a cough. Ruth was in the kitchen putting a salve on Red Monroe's foot fungus. It didn't seem right to leave that pie's sweet goodness next to that business, so I squeezed me and the pie through the door to the pantry.

There must have been a dozen jars. Once I was in the pantry, I saw that the sun had beaten me there. Fingers of light reached through cracks in the log wall to touch the glass wombs. They sparked and sparkled like dry kindle on fire. Ruth made me swear not to tell anyone what I'd seen. She said she didn't have it in her to let those babies get thrown away. I never told her secret to a soul who would repeat it. Ruth loved me for it. She was a peculiar one, that Ruth, but she felt like home to me.

| MAMA TRAPPED DADDY |

I stole away to the barn around sundown one evening late that fall, soon as I finished my chores. My plan was to spend some time reading before Mama called me for supper. My eyes hardly touched words on the page before I saw Ruth through the hayloft's open doors. She was coming from across our west field, strolling pretty as you please with a line of squirrels in the grip of one hand and a mass of purple ironweed in the other. The sunlight behind her yellow hair lent her the look of one of those haloed saints from the Renaissance paintings I'd seen in an art book at the Luray library. Only Ruth's torn coat and brown calico dress gave her away as mountain folk.

She stopped before she got to the barn, out at the hog pen's fence line, and searched the ground for something. In a moment, she dropped the flowers and picked up a rock, which she chucked through the open hay loft doors right at me. "Jesus Ruth!" She'd managed to peg me in the arm. "Bee?" She whispered loud as she could and have it still be a whisper. "You in there?"

"Yes I'm in here," I said. "You nailed me with that goddamned rock."

"Sorry," she said. She hid her mouth behind her hand. I didn't have to see her smile to know she was a little tickled that her rock had found me in the shadowy hayloft. "I can't make you out. Your Mama in there?"

"No. She's in the house. Come on up."

"No can do, Busy Bee. We gotta get a move on. You come on down." She picked her flowers up off the ground and trotted through the gate, into the barn.

Soon as my last foot left the loft ladder, Ruth handed me the pretty purple flowers. I must have looked flummoxed because she spelled it out for me. "I done brought 'em for you. And these." She shoved the line of squirrels, three tied together, at me. "Hide 'em in the hay loft. Go run tell your Mama you're going squirrel hunting with me. Give her these soon as we get back so she won't doubt you."

The squirrels were no surprise. Ruth could hit a bounding rabbit with one rifle shot from a hundred paces. She'd lived my seventeen years, plus seventeen more. That was enough time that she had to kill her share of critters or starve. She couldn't abide suffering though. She'd nurse back to health any living thing that was hurt, long as it wasn't needed for supper. She saved a three-legged skunk from bleeding to death once after it lost its fourth leg to a hunter's trap. That animal never sprayed her, but it covered her husband Peter in its stink plenty.

The flowers were unexpected though. I asked her what in God's name I was supposed to do with them. I certainly wasn't giving those pretty things to Mama, nasty as she'd been.

"They'll make you happy to look at 'em," Ruth said.

I asked Ruth where this place was that we were going that was special enough to make her go to all this trouble to cover our tracks. "It ain't the where, it's the how." Her eyes grew big. "I got us a car." She was whispering again, like too much noise might wake us up from this good dream. She reached out and took hold of my hand so hard the squirrels swung wildly, dead trapeze artists on a string. "I got us a car with a radio!"

Just about every car you come across in the city these days has a radio in it. But up mountain, nobody had radios since they cost more than the old jalopies around there were worth. I'd heard the old men down at MacArthur's say the DeKalbs bought a Deluxe Model A with a hundred-dollar Motorola in it. They were a family that lived down between Livingston and Nicholson Hollows and, as far as folks around the Hollow were concerned, they were rich as the Rockefellers. They sold the apples they grew to somebody in England who bought them for what I heard tell was as much as eight thousand dollars one year.

The DeKalbs felt like they owed Ruth since she pulled their boy Rupert from the stony cold grip of the Grim Reaper himself when an influenza epidemic had spread across four hollows years before. Death stayed busy for a good six weeks carrying off the too young and the too old. Three-year-old Rupert was close to pushing up daisies when Mr. DeKalb sent for Ruth. She made that boy drink enough black elder flower tea to drown a possum and in a few days he was good as new. Mr. DeKalb offered Ruth some obscene sum of money that embarrassed her so terribly she never would tell me how much it was. She refused it. In fact, she treated a right good many people during that epidemic and never did take a dime from anyone. It wouldn't have been right, she said, to take people's money under the circumstances.

When Ruth came to get me that evening, she said I'd been down in the mouth about that Rowler business for too long. She'd been thinking hard on a way to cheer me up. It came to her that a ride in the DeKalbs' car might just do the trick. I'm sure when she asked, Mr. DeKalb handed the keys over without hesitation.

After I sold Mama the squirrel hunting story, Ruth led me to the road to Mountaintop where she'd parked the car. What a car! Shining black as freshly polished boots, with two big headlights round as owl eyes. Leather seats buffed smooth enough for a Queen's ass to take a seat. The Motorola radio puffed its chest out from the dash, proud of its reputation as a thing glorious and rare as gold dust.

Ruth started her up. She and Peter had a pickup she ran around in regularly, so she had enough experience to be a relaxed driver. Neither one of us touched the radio until we were at the bottom of the mountain. Ruth turned the dial slowly, carefully, until it clicked on. It only screeched static at first. I pushed buttons until my fingers found a record I would have picked myself if I'd been at the turntable. The radio station's man said the singer was a negress songbird named Holiday and the song was called "The Very Thought of You."

We rode through the dark without speaking, while that Holiday bird went on singing in a way that sounded a lot like crying to me, but it was beautiful just the same. Being a love story set to music, naturally it made me think of Miles. I started dreaming of the night we swam in Miller's pond in the altogether. He kissed me on the shore first. I bit his lip so hard he let out a shout and let me go, but it must not have bothered him too much because he was after me again soon as I hit the water. In the car with Ruth, I secretly recalled wrapping my legs around him in the pond that night, the first time we were together. It gave me a tiny thrill to think of it. A heartache followed at the thought of not seeing Miles again until he crossed the country twice -- away, then back to me.

More songs played on the Motorola. Ruth and I kept on not talking.

There was plenty we could have said, but running our mouths would have been nothing special. When you have someone you can be quiet with, now that is something.

I rolled my window part way down. I stuck my hand out and let the wind buffet my arm, first up then down, depending on which way I turned my fingers. Up ahead we could see the lighted windows of Sperryile's general store moving up to meet us. Ruth parked the car in front. A few locals stopped to ogle it. They looked fit to be tied when we stepped out of it, Ruth in her faded calico dress and me in my coveralls. They must have thought us part of the Barrow gang since we two surely couldn't have got the keys to such a beautiful machine without sticking somebody up for them. We bought two bottles of Coca-Cola in the store. The man behind the counter opened them for us. We looked around while we sipped their bubbling sweetness, compared the store to our MacArthur's, then decided folks in Sperryville would be better off driving up our way to shop.

When we came out again, a lawman was standing beside the car. He had a lot of questions about who it belonged to and how Ruth came to be driving it. I told him about the DeKalbs and Ruth's influenza cure. After a long questioning, he decided to let us go. At the time I thought it was an adventure to be at odds with the law, even if it was only for a little while.

Ruth and I had a good laugh on the way home about it. Once we were done giggling, Ruth got real serious. She said Mama has a secret and it was about time I knew it.

"You was born five months after your folks got hitched," Ruth said. "I reckon you're grown enough to hear it now. She married your daddy 'cause she'd done got herself stuck." I opened my mouth to talk, but Ruth held up her hand and kept going. "There ain't a soul alive who don't see how bad she treats you. You ain't earned it, Busy Bee. You got to know that. I'd bet a week's worth of milk she's sore 'cause she never could go back to the city. I sworn, that woman blamed a child when she stepped in a snare with her own foot."

It was a shock to hear my own Mama and Daddy had a shotgun wedding. Even though I had sure enough rolled in the hay with Miles and not been married to him, it was altogether different to picture my prim and proper Mama doing it. That and the shame of knowing everybody could see that my own Mama hated me made me want to go back to shopping in the Sperryville store, before I knew how close I'd come to getting myself born a bastard child and despised to boot.

We rode in silence again like before, but this time Ruth's news made the air heavy. Half way home, I had a revelation of my own.

"Ruth, that can't be," I said.

"What you mean, hon?"

"Mama can't have gone and gotten herself knocked up by accident. You've said it yourself before: she's the most orderly woman you know. She kept the school in firewood even when nobody went to class anymore. Hell, she tracks our sow's monthlies on the calendar so we know when to breed her. She'd never make a mistake that big."

"Even your Mama might get carried away," Ruth said. "A man handsome as your Daddy could make a woman forget herself."

"Mama's never gotten carried away in her life," I said.

"What you figure happened?"

It only took a minute for the answer to come to me, and I was sure of it as I was that the sun would rise again the next day. "She tricked him," I said.

"Bee. Your Mama'd give her eye teeth to get free of this mountain. Why on God's green earth would she go and stick herself here?"

"She had me before the blight, right?"

"Yeah."

"Daddy's family had money then," I said. "They had an account at that tannery down in Luray. Remember? They used to sell chestnut bark by the truck load."

"Uh huh." Ruth sounded uncertain.

"Don't you see it Ruth? The state only paid her for a year. Folks here kept her on, but they couldn't pay her near as much. She had to find a husband. And the blight didn't kill the trees until I was a girl so, when she married Daddy, Mama thought she'd done well for herself."

"She could've went back to her people in Richmond."

"Her daddy was dead as a doornail by then. Her ma got remarried to a prick named Virgil who hates Mama almost as much as she hates him. I expect Mama'd rather hang herself from a chestnut tree than live with him."

Ruth chewed on this for a while, then said, "I done put it out of my mind 'til now, but about nine months before you was born your Mama and Daddy was on the outs, then got back together real sudden like. Him and my oldest brother was talking one night over a jug of white mule. I remember 'cause I was a young pup in love when it come to your Daddy. He was a little too old for me, but I hung close whenever he was around just the same. I heard him say he and your Mama had gotten themselves into a fix. He said they needed to get hitched in a hurry. He was real torn up about it but she skipped 'round here pleased as punch."

"I'll be goddamned," I said. I knew I was right, but Ruth's proof of it threw me.

Mama must have wanted me to do the same as her and sleep with a man I didn't love to fix my future. She was out of her gourd if she thought I was going to pull my pants down for Rowler. Right then, I started working up the courage to say something to her about tricking Daddy. I wasn't going to be forced into making her mistakes.

Other than that business about Mama and Daddy, it was a good night. Ruth set out to lift my spirits, and for a while they soared high as a kite on a windy day.

THAT THIEVING RED MONROE STEALS DADDY'S WORM

The promise of money enough to change my circumstances had a pull too powerful to ignore. I had Daddy's still up and running a few weeks after Buddy suggested it. Daddy first set it up back before I was born, next to an arm of Brokenback Run. It was still there, all except for the worm. It occurs to me that you may not know what a worm is. It's the magical copper coil that turns a whole bunch of steam into whiskey a man can drink. Daddy's had gone missing, but I knew who had it. Daddy was known to make the best moonshine in the Hollow. That swindler Red Monroe had sabotaged Daddy's still more than once and stole his customers while Daddy was out of business.

I walked the five miles to Red's house before noon the day I saw the worm was gone. When I got there, it was just his wife Sarah and their youngest John at the house. Sarah and Red had five boys who Sarah named for the apostles after a traveling preacher gave her a painting of the Last Supper. She named them just as those holy men appeared at the table in the painting, left to right. Their oldest boy was Bartholomew, then came James, Andrew and Peter. Sarah had the good sense to skip Judas and go straight to John for their youngest. I checked the painting while I was there -- it was hung lopsided above the fireplace. It looked to me like if they had another one, they would have had to name him Jesus.

I waited for Red for hours. I had a hunch he saw me coming and hightailed it out of there. He was probably watching from a tree like a scared 'coon for me to go. My guess was he wanted to keep that worm for himself. I knew as well as anybody copper coils didn't come free.

Sarah had a devout pleasantness about her. She was all soft corners and fluttery words, like she'd been wrapped in gauze. It soothed me to be around her, so I stayed and helped her sweep the porch and clean the dead leaves and sticks out of the yard. Then we fixed some navy beans with a ham hock that'd already been stewed so many times there was only bone left. I made the cornbread and the coffee while Sarah mended clothes torn by work or the boys' roughhousing. I watched her sew runaway buttons back on their cotton keepers, order restored.

It was nice to have a break from Mama. She'd been on a tear about everything that had to do with me. A few nights earlier, I'd left the door to the chicken coop open while I ran back to the house to get the supper scraps I meant to feed the birds. She saw what I'd done and read me the riot act about how a fox would have killed every chicken we had that night while my pretty little head was sleeping on a chicken feather pillow. When I argued that I was only gone a minute, she shooed and kicked every one of those chickens out of that coop and told me I had a quarter hour to get them back in or I'd be sleeping with them. Goddamn, son-of-a-bitching chickens scattered so far afield there was no way I could catch them all in time. I wanted to break every one of their scrawny, little chicken necks.

But I was telling you about my visit to Red and Sarah's. My thoughts are scattered as those damnable chickens. I had to get home before dark came, so I asked Sarah when I might catch Red. She had the idea that I could find him at church on Sunday. Evidently, she told Red that he'd go to church Sunday or not lay with her again until he got right with the Lord. We had a traveling preacher who only came around once a year. If talk around the Hollow was true and Sarah only screwed Red on Christmas and his May birthday, I knew with Christmas coming up that Red's ass would be in those pews come hell or high water.

Sunday, I got to church right as Pastor Easton cracked open his bible. Sure enough, there was Red at the end of the third pew in pants he must have borrowed from one of his sons. The extra length was cuffed at the bottom on account of the fact that every one of his boys was taller than him, except the youngest who was about even then and him only a kid. I slid in next to Red, dropped my head and pretended to pray. But instead of Our Father, I whispered, "I know you've got it you son of a bitch."

Red shifted in his seat. He folded his hands under his chin and whispered back that he didn't know what I was talking about. This went on for a minute or two before Sarah elbowed Red in the ribs. Red tried a new tack: he didn't know who had stolen my worm, but he'd be happy to sell me a spare one he had for two dollars.

You might have thought Red would offer up the worm with his condolences for Daddy's passing. I'll remind you that Red was crooked as a dog's hind leg.

If Red wanted to play hardball, I was game. I told him if he didn't have that worm to me before the day was out, I'd tell Sarah he'd been sampling so much of his own product he didn't have any left to sell. Sarah didn't mind Red brewing whiskey if it put food on the table, but she didn't cotton to his drinking it. I said I'd wait until Pastor Easton was gone, so he'd have to spend a long while in a cold bed before he could ask God's forgiveness. Red agreed to my terms right away.

After the service, Pastor Easton cornered me and Red. Up close I could see the pastor's hair was slicked back with too much pomade -- might as well have greased his head with chicken fat. His hands rubbed together like two kids courting. He eyed me and Red good and said he'd be making the rounds for donations soon. Instead of a regular paycheck, the pastor collected whatever Hollow folk had to pay him with: eggs, milk, apple butter. But his far and away favorite donation was a jug of mountain moonshine. He said it helped him commune with the Holy Spirit and God wouldn't frown on that. Sarah must have overheard him because she sidled up to Red quick as you please and said Red was working on a batch just for Pastor Easton. The pastor's eyes brightened. Red sort of gasped, "You mean the whole batch?" She said it was just what Red needed to get him right with God and that was the end of that.

|ROWLER POUNCES|

I went to Mountaintop a few times to sell my whiskey before I wised up and caught on that my poor little mountain girl routine didn't work with whiskey like it did when I sold my baskets of berries. Women bought baskets, men bought booze. It occurred to me that it might help if I vamped it up a bit. I put on the green calico dress Daddy had bought to match my eyes when I was fifteen. It was tight enough two years later that men couldn't help but notice I'd grown up. I dragged a brush through my hair. I sneaked the Red Raspberry Max Factor lipstick out of Mama's vanity table drawer. She'd had it for years, so all that was left was a waxy rim around the inside of the metal tube. It made hollow red circles on my lips when I pressed it to them. I spread the color with my finger, then smudged what was left on my cheeks.

I packed mason jars full of whiskey into burlap sacks filled with enough leaves to keep them from smashing each other to pieces, then I loaded our old mule Molly up with the bags. I took the long way so Molly and I could cut over to the fire road instead of walking the rocky creek bed like I usually did. Since Molly'd gotten long in the tooth, her footing wasn't as sure as it used to be. It was before supper, so not pitch black yet, but the sun was giving out from a day's work. In its lazy light, I saw Red Monroe walking back to his daddy's truck. He used it to haul his whiskey up the mountain, then parked half a mile from Mountaintop, where the guests wouldn't see, and carried the jars in on his back like the city folks' idea of a poor mountain man. I wasn't the only one who'd figured out how to pull the wool over the city folks' eyes.

He took one look at me and said, "Your Daddy'd turn over'n his grave he knew you were 'bout to go up yonder to Buddy's place looking like that." I told Red to mind his own damn business. I was old enough to look out for myself. "I guess you are," he said, then aimed a wad of tobacco juice at the dirt but hit his boot with it instead. "Goddammit. Sarah just done shined these this morning." He wiped his boot on the back of his pants leg, took another look at me and said, "Suit yourself." He was making tracks before Molly and I had gone a step further.

A minute later a black Ford roadster tore around a curve in the road. It kicked up enough dust to choke a person. When it pulled up alongside me and Molly, I saw it was Rowler in the driver's seat. He hollered something at me. I couldn't make out what. Then he stopped and leaned out the truck window, close enough that I could smell Red's cheap whiskey on him. He asked me if I was alone, to which I answered "a blind man could see that I am." He laughed without smiling.

Rowler said I looked pretty as a picture. I might as well have been naked as a jaybird for the way he looked at me. I knew it wasn't possible, but I could have sworn I felt his eyeballs crawling up under my dress. I said I needed to be getting on to Mountaintop, so I'd have to excuse myself. I heard him grind the truck into reverse. He coaxed the gas pedal just enough to stick beside me and Molly. He started talking to me in the kind of low voice Daddy would use to soothe a chicken he was after for the frying pan. "Pretty girl like you shouldn't be out alone this late. You're asking for trouble." He wanted to know if I'd ever been to a picture show. I said no even though Daddy'd taken me to see The Man Who Knew Too Much before he died. I didn't want to give Rowler a reason to hang around and chat.

It was about this time I decided to hell with Mountaintop -- I'd turn around for home. No sooner had Molly and I turned than he put the car back in drive and eased it alongside us again. I led Molly into the woods. The underbrush was so thick we couldn't go in deep, but at least we were off the road. If I had to, I could leave Molly and try to lose Rowler on my own. From my place in the trees, I could still see him in the windows of light that opened between the black trunks. I guess he could see me too because he shouted that he'd seen a Fred Astaire movie that made him think of me. He stepped onto the road and let the truck keep rolling beside him. He started hopping from foot to foot next to it like a crazy man, dancing with a pretend partner, singing in a queer voice:

"Whether near to me or far

It's no matter, darling, where you are

I think of you day and night."

I tripped on a tree root in my hurry to get away from him. When I looked to the road, I could only see that bastard's empty truck rolled to a stop in the middle of it. He'd stepped into the trees somewhere behind me. He started whooping so loud the sound of it bounced around and made it near about impossible for me to tell where he was. Right about the time it dawned on me I was in real trouble, he jumped from behind a curtain of pine boughs and grabbed ahold of my skirt's hem. I tried like hell to pull away. There was no shaking him. All my twisting and turning only landed me on my ass in the leaves.

He was on all fours over my ankles before I could blink. His fingers were still clamped down on my hem. He spun his hand in circles until my dress was wrapped around it. Every other piece of clothing I owned would have let me tear myself free. Not that dress. It was made from good, strong fabric Daddy paid a pretty penny for, not knowing it would tether me to a monster someday. Rowler crawled up me, his own felled tree, pulling the bottom of my dress up with him.

A car horn hooted from the road. Another car was passing, no doubt on its way to Mountaintop. I was Andromeda, the driver my Perseus -- honking and yelling for the jackass who was blocking the road to come get his car. Rowler looked down at me before he trotted back to the road. He said, "'til we meet again" and tipped a pretend hat in my direction.

After he got in his truck and drove down the mountain, I turned Molly back toward Mountaintop. It was closer than home and I wanted lights and people. Before that day I felt safe in the Hollow. After it, there were more parts than not where I felt exposed, like even the woods had turned on me.

The resort was packed to the hilt with rabble-rousers. It wasn't even suppertime yet, but Buddy had already worked the guests into a frenzy with firecrackers and whiskey. He was in rare form, dressed as an Arabian knight, spurring General until he reared. Molly was so jittery from all the commotion, I had to put my hand on her neck to calm her down. That ought to tell you something about how wild it was, because mules don't tend to have the same nervous temperaments as finer horses.

I emptied some of the leaves out of my bags of moonshine glass so, when Molly walked, they'd clink loud enough to advertise for us. I fluffed myself up and pinched my cheeks, since I figured my run in with Rowler had made the blood run right out of them. I sold most of what I brought before I made it halfway around the cabins. Every time a firecracker's glow lit me up, the men would elbow each other and come stumbling over. They were all so drunk already I couldn't imagine why they wanted more. I'll bet their aching heads made them wish for death the next day.   Red was right. Daddy wouldn't have wanted me in the middle of that scene. But I was right too. I took plenty good care of myself. I felt a man's hand on me more than once. I told each of them they'd better move it or lose it. For extra measure, I lied and said I had a hulking sweetheart with a temper big enough to blow through that mountain out west they were cutting the presidents' faces into, and that he was keeping an eye on me from the woods. Then I'd wave and holler, "Hey sweetheart!"

As I tucked the night's haul (fifteen dollars!) into one of the almost-empty burlap sacks, I heard someone holler at me from across the lawn. It was Buddy in full Arabian glory. He had on a white robe with a silver sash tied around his bulging stomach and a headdress that flowed like water over his shoulders. He looked like the bride at a shotgun wedding. He was on foot, a fact which I'm sure poor General was glad of, with a woman I couldn't quite make out at his side. "Whoo girl!" He was still shouting even though he'd gotten close enough for me to hear him at a loud whisper. "You're sure all grown up." That's when I saw the face of the woman at his side. It was Mama. She looked fit to be tied which, I knew, didn't bode well for me.

She studied Buddy who studied me. He was grunting like a man who wanted to move his bowels but couldn't. Mama asked Buddy to excuse us so she could have a word with me. He trotted back toward the crowd.

Mama was just about the last person I expected to see up at Mountaintop. You could have knocked me over with a chicken feather. I was still trying to get my head straight when she wrapped her fingers around my upper arm and squeezed hard enough to leave black and blue fingerprints. "If you know what's good for you," she said through her teeth, "you'll go home and wipe that lipstick of your face. No daughter of mine is going to be seen selling liquor with her face made up like a clown's."

I pulled my arm away. Catching Mama somewhere she wasn't supposed to be had made me bold. "Why are you so worried about what people are going to think of me? You're the one on Buddy's arm."

"I wasn't on his arm," she said. "Mr. Collins invited me here for dinner and I accepted as his companion."

"Have you forgotten he killed Daddy?"

"That was an accident. Besides, Mr. Collins is a man of means, and he could use a refined woman to help him host his city guests. I'm hopeful he and I can come to some arrangement. In the meantime, I won't have you ruining things with all this carrying on like a common whore."

After Mama let loose of my arm, I headed for home. I wiped off what was left of the lipstick on the way. Mama'd made me embarrassed to wear it. I crawled into bed and pretended to be asleep a few hours later when I heard her at the door. Pretty soon, I was dreaming about the fifteen dollars I'd made.

| MAMA TEARS UP THE STILL |

Mama tore up the still. I tiptoed into the kitchen to put the coffee on the morning after I ran into her at Mountaintop and saw the worm, the magical copper coil that was going to earn me my way out of the Hollow, laying hammered and bent on the table. I guess she was mad enough to find the still in the dark. I stared at the worm for a good minute. I knew it wasn't a living thing, but I was sad about its passing just the same.

Then Mama spoke to me from her rocker by the fireplace. She was never up before me in the morning, so the sound of her voice gave me a start. She said she couldn't see how selling bootleg whiskey at Mountaintop was better than letting that nice state man woo me.

I told her about what happened the night before -- Rowler's fingers choking the hem of my dress. "He's not Daddy," I said. "He won't be tricked into marrying me."

She made a big fuss about how she didn't know what I was talking about. When I told her I knew she'd hidden a belly full of baby me under her wedding dress, she said so what. Accidents happen. What mattered was that Daddy did the right thing.

"You knew he would," I said. "I wasn't an accident. You tricked a good man into marrying you to fix your own future and now you think I should do it too -- except Rowler's not a good man and I'm not a liar."

She flew at me from her rocker. She smacked me in the back of my head after I shielded my face with my arms. She said for me to give her the money. She sort of snarled it at me through her teeth so I knew she meant business.

Hollow kids would sometimes bend saplings to the ground, sit on the tops, then let go. When the trees snapped back into place, they sure could send a body for a wild ride. As soon as I heard Mama say the word money, I felt like I'd been flung from a sapling straight toward a rock wall. In my head I flailed for something to grab ahold of. I asked Mama what money to gain the benefit of time.

She pushed past me into my room. She flung my clothes from their homes in my dresser drawers. My undergarments blew around the room like leaves. She pushed my mattress onto the floor. She found one of my Billy Faulkner books and ripped its pages right out. This was too much for me. I gave in too soon and told her I'd stuffed the money inside my mattress. When she found it, she put it in her apron pocket. I begged her not to take it, but she took no pity on me. She looked me square in the eyes and said she wished I'd never been born. I'm sorry to say my defenses didn't hold up to that one. My eyes let go of about a hundred tears. For my part, I wish I hadn't been born such a weak girl that a few spoken words could have such an effect on me.

Mama made it her day's work to take me down a few pegs. She told me to put my green dress back on (she said if I liked it so much I could live in it). I wore it to feed the animals, clean out the barn and the spring house, weed all six acres of the garden, beat the dust out of the rugs and blankets. By the end of the day, the only nice dress I owned was so stained and torn it looked like a pack of wild dogs had their way with it.

| THE OUTLAW SHEP JONES |

In the middle of it all, I went fishing with Torch and Red to take my mind off of Rowler and missing Miles. You may think I should have given Red the cold shoulder after all that business with the worm. There was no point in holding it against him. Thievery was in his nature. Besides, I figured someday somebody would shoot him or hang him one, and that would be his comeuppance.

Red would always bring his own fishing pole when we all went together, but that was all. He sneaked the worms Torch dug and he sipped from my jars of white mule. He was good fun on a fishing trip, though. He could be counted on for a laugh, usually at someone else's expense. That day it was Torch's turn.

The best fish were at Miller's pond, down mountain a good way. We crossed Brokenback Run at its deepest point to get there. If we crossed too soon, we'd have to fight our way through a briar patch. The three of us decided we'd rather tiptoe across slippery rocks and risk a fall in the cold water than get caught in the arms of those prickly, scrambling bushes. On the way there, Red crossed first. Then he and I held opposite ends of his fishing pole to make a line for Torch to grab onto while he made his way to the other side. Red and I were sure-footed on the creek's wet-rock stepping stones, but Torch always wobbled. That day, Torch's bag was loaded down with the day's food and bait. His heavy load made him sway more than usual, but he held tight to the pole and kept his feet under him.

I didn't dare tell Torch about my troubles with Rowler. I was afraid he'd fight for me like a mama bear for her cub. Rowler was big, but Torch could be fierce when it came to me, so he might have gained the upper hand. Beating a government man to a pulp probably would have landed him behind bars. I didn't need that on my conscience. Besides, it was nice to spend a day in peace. I didn't once have to hear that man's name spoken out loud.

We had a picnic while we were fishing. You could catch them at Miller's pond even in winter, you just had to weigh down the hook to make it sink to the bottom where those fish lazed around when it was cold. We finished a jar of white mule between the three of us and ate the fried fatback and sweet pickles Torch brought from his Daddy's store. Then Red, who it could be argued had no talent other than to act a fool, came around to the topic of the government taking our land and sending us all down the mountain. It wasn't long before he made one of his usual pea-brained comments. "Outlaw Jones'll have to wear a disguise if he goes down mountain," he said. "He oughta blacken his face with coal and pretend to be a Negro."

Red said this with a straight face, and the ridiculousness of it made us laugh. "You goddamned idiot," Torch said, still laughing. "You think folks ain't gonna figure that out? What's he gonna do if it rains?"

I don't suppose I've told you about the Outlaw Shep Jones yet. He showed up in the Hollow with his wife at the start of 1894. They had two sons after that, but they stayed a mystery since they generally didn't mix with us mountain folks. In fact, Jones made it known anybody who so much as tried to take his photograph or stare at him long enough to recreate his likeness would get himself shot square between the eyes. On the rare occasion when I came across him in the woods, he pulled his hat down so low it was a wonder he could see where he was headed.

The hat he wore was a Homburg. I certainly didn't consider myself knowledgeable about men's hats, but I had seen one that matched his in a magazine ad that said, "The St. Louis Homburg, $3.50." It was black felt with a black grosgrain band. Before Jones, and then the one in the magazine, I'd never seen one like it. Mountain men didn't much go in for felt hats. If you'd asked me, it was a dead giveaway Jones was from a city somewhere far off and laying low where he thought nobody would look. Folks around the Hollow had their theories. Some said he was part of the James-Younger gang -- unlikely since those boys put down their guns in 1880 and Jones didn't show up in the Hollow until fourteen years later. No, I always thought the theory that held the most water was the one that said Jones played a part in a Missouri train robbery at the tail end of 1893.

The way I heard it told, a Southern Railway train was boarded by six bandits just outside Poplar Bluff after it stopped for a downed tree on the tracks. The passengers and the train strongbox were robbed and the engineer was killed in a shootout. The robbers escaped. Later, four of them were tracked down by posses hired by the railroad. All four of those men were hanged. But what of the other two? Virginia would have been a long haul from Missouri, but the railroad probably hung wanted posters with the bandits' likenesses in every post office west of the Mississippi. That made Virginia a good choice for a hideout.

The Outlaw Jones might not have been the only man who went to the Hollow to hide. There was more than one man rumored to have been a Confederate renegade. But you should know most folks who settled there were good, God-fearing people who were after better lives for their families.

After we were done laughing at Red, Torch wandered off to take a piss. Soon as he was gone, Red pulled out a handkerchief. Its wrinkled center held a glob of lard. Red rubbed it up and down his fishing pole's middle. Then he winked at me.

You might guess where this story is going. You might wonder why I didn't stop Red, or say something to Torch. Well, Torch had played more than a few pranks on me, so I figured what's good for the goose ...

When it came time to cross Brokenback Run, Red and I held on to the ends of his fishing pole like before. We'd eaten enough at lunch to lighten Torch's bags considerably, but he'd also had half a jar of white mule. As soon as his hands got to the greased part of the pole, he lost hold. He was flat on his ass in no time, chest deep in that cold December water before he knew what hit him. He cursed up a storm. He called us "Goddamned son of a bitching mother fuckers!" He got up, then fell back in a few times. He called us some other names I couldn't make out because I was laughing so hard.

Torch shivered all the way back to MacArthur's. It took him a half hour in front of the wood stove before he could stop his teeth chattering. Soon as he could talk without sounding like a typewriter he said thanks to me and Red, he damn near about froze his pecker off. I told him I didn't see what the big deal was since it didn't get much use. He called me some more names. They were pretty funny but for once I'll be lady enough not to put them to paper.

Once he'd warmed up enough to negotiate, we made a deal. He wouldn't scheme to get back at me if I'd agree to help him prank Red. I did. The next day, I stood lookout just north of the outhouse behind Red's place while Torch hid in the bushes behind it. Torch didn't dare peek out from the bushes and risk giving himself away. My job was to perch myself in a pine (those goddamned needles were prickly as hell). As soon as Red stepped into the necessary house, I was to let loose with my best sparrow whistle. Torch would know Red was about to pull down his britches.

Before I finish my story, I have to tell you something you may not know: Red was scared to death of finding a snake in the shitter. He told us once he'd had dreams about a copperhead rising up out of the foul blackness underneath the seat and biting him on his ass. Now you know where Torch got his inspiration.

So back to the outhouse. At my call, Torch jammed the end of a piece of barbed wire through a hole between the shitter's wood slats. Just as Torch planned, the wire hit Red hard in one of his butt cheeks. Red busted out of there like his ass was on fire. His pants were still down around his ankles and his jigglestick was bouncing around like a jack in the box head on an accordion spring. His voice was high as a girl's and he was hooting and hollering, "I been bit! I been bit! Lord spare me!" It was one of the better laughs I'd had in a long time. I hope it tickles you to read about it.

| ROWLER BEATS TWO SILASES |

It wasn't long after spending such a carefree day with Torch and Red that I saw Rowler again. This time his men were beating Big Si Barnes to a bloody pulp. I watched Big Si's namesake and oldest son Silas Junior, who I had necked with a few summers before, carry his little brother Eddie to a seat in their wagon before he dove into the brawl and took a beating too.

I was on a hunt for Bessie, our knocked-up sow. She'd birthed a few litters by then. She got ants in her pants every time she was preggers -- knocked a hole in the fence so she could wander. I'm not sure why. Maybe the feel of all those little piglets wriggling inside her made her want to move too. She almost always headed south by southeast, so that's where I tracked her. Soon as I was within earshot of the Barnes' place, I heard Big Si hollering the longest line of curse words anybody ever strung together.

From my spot at the edge of the clearing that circled their house, I saw Big Si standing on his porch, heads above the three men standing four steps down in his yard. They were government men. I could tell by the crisp newness of their shirts. The one in the middle was Rowler. He was a foot in front of the other two, pack leader. Big Si shouted something about this being his land and he wasn't leaving it. No way, no how. He threatened to get his rifle and blow their crooked government asses off his property if they didn't leave on their own steam. That was all Rowler needed. He nodded his head at his two goons, who had Big Si between them in a flash. They dragged Big Si down the steps. He thrashed loose of their hold. He threw a few punches before one landed. Then they were on him again, only this time he'd given them a reason to get rough.

He called for Silas to get little Eddie and Mrs. Barnes to safety. Mrs. Barnes was already in the wagon. Silas ran Eddie over and put him in the seat beside her. Then he did what I'm sure was the last thing Big Si wanted: he ran back over to defend his daddy. Only he didn't come back empty handed -- he brought the horsewhip from the wagon. One crack of that whip was all it took to turn the goons on him.

Mrs. Barnes commenced screaming bloody murder. Little Eddie cried out for them to leave his brother alone. I should have picked up a stick and run out to help, but the scene shocked me into stillness.

Big Si rose up from where they'd pinned him on the ground, his nose spurting blood, to help his boy. Things went from bad to worse. Rowler's men had blackjacks in their belts. I guess the fight was too close to fair for their liking, because they drew those batons and let loose. They walloped Big Si and Silas more than once. It took the sound of Big Si's arm cracking in two for the men to stop. If they hadn't called it quits on their own, I'm not sure Rowler would have stopped them. He was cold-blooded, that one.

Both Silases had faces streaked with blood. Silas Junior helped his daddy to the wagon. They walked, heads down, beaten. Mrs. Barnes and Eddie were crying. It hurt me to see it, so I turned away.

| DISAPPEARING HOUSES |

It was before Christmas when Torch found out about the disappearing houses. He came up to the barn one night to tell me. I was mucking stalls. It had been so cold I'd been bringing the animals in at night, which created a lot more work for me than if they did their business outside. Torch grabbed a pitch fork and helped. While we worked he told me about meeting Red on his way up mountain the day before. You remember thieving Red Monroe, who stole my Daddy's worm and his own dead Mama's hair? Torch caught him with sticky fingers again. This time it was the Holcomb's door. Papa Holcomb had it made out of pure Virginia pine at a sawmill ten years before, then added a carving he made himself of a dogwood blossom. It was a nice piece of craftsmanship. There must have been a dozen gawkers there the day Holcomb hung it. There wasn't a soul among us who didn't admire that wooden blossom especially. It looked soft as a real flower, but it was all wood, solid to the touch.

The Holcomb family was one of the first to move into resettlement housing. When the younger Holcombs asked Papa if he wanted to cart the door down to the new house, he told them the door belonged on the mountain. Between puffs on his pipe, he said, "Something that pretty'd be out of place on one of them ugly boxes the government calls houses." The Holcombs told him it was just as well, that flowered door would be waiting for them when the government let them come back to their Hollow home. Torch said the day the government let us back the devil would have to wrap himself in a wool blanket to keep out the cold in Hell and the rest of us would be ducking flying donkeys.

Nevertheless, I'm sure Papa and the rest of the Holcomb family would have had fits if they knew Red made off with that door. Torch told me Red had it half off its hinges when he saw him. "Goddammit Red,"

Torch said. "Don't you have any respect? You were here the day Papa Holcomb hung that door. You drank his white mule and carried on about his carving skills."

"I sure 'nuff did," Red said. "And I must've meant it, or I wouldn't be stealing this here door, would I?" Red went on to justify his thievery by repeating Torch's very own words back to him. "You're the one tellin' everybody it'll be a cold day in hell 'fore they let us back here. Don't do no good to leave this stuff."

"I don't expect they'll let us live here again," Torch said, "but we can leave our mark. Don't you want the city folks who tour around these woods to know that men lived here once strong enough to carve homesteads out of a mountainside?"

Red hawked one of the giant gobs of tobacco spit he's known for in Torch's direction. "It hurts me awful bad to tell you this, friend," he said. "But they done erased a dozen of our so-called marks already and they're fixin' to level this whole place."

"What in blue blazes are you talking about?"

"Those rangers've bulldozed a bunch of houses down Corbin Hollow way. Even leveled a few grave sites they came across. I figure they gonna be flattening places up here in a week's time." Red rubbed his hands together. He rested his eyes on that prized door. "I say grab what you can 'fore these woods get turned back over to God. I play my cards right, I can steal me enough pieces to make a whole house somewhere else."

That night after Mama fell asleep, I sneaked out of the house to meet Torch. We headed down to Corbin Hollow in the dark to see if what Red said was true. There was some moonlight and, anyway, we know our way around the hollows well enough to walk blindfolded. Red was right. In clearings where houses used to stand, only scraps were left. The Mason place, the Haner's and the Scruder's had all been razed. Disappeared. Only the Hardwick house was still standing. The inside glowed with lantern and fire light. Through the windows, we could see the government's park rangers eating and drinking at the Hardwick's table. The Hardwicks weren't there. The day Rowler delivered the notice of government seizure, Mr. Hardwick went out to his barn and hung himself from the rafters. Mrs. Hardwick and the younger kids went off to Sperryville to live with her oldest son and his new wife.

. . .

It snowed on the mountain on Christmas Eve that year. In places, the drifts were high enough to hide a goat. I couldn't sleep for missing Miles, so I went out in it. The snow made a wet sound when it landed, like soggy cotton would. It made my soul feel restful. Everything stopped while it was falling. The whole world counting flakes. When the snow was done and the sky cleared, the moon started showing off -- bouncing its beams off the ice crystals, lighting up the night like it was day. The sun would've been jealous.

After my midnight walk, I went to the barn. I used to go there to read books Mama didn't approve of. I hid them in the hayloft. I hauled the hay up and threw a few flakes down at feeding time, so Mama never went up there. On Christmas Eve, I decided to climb up to the loft to read until my eyes got tired. When I opened the barn door, I saw something I didn't expect. A she-wolf was standing in the aisle, straight from Dante's hell, with human eyes and a heavy coat, red and black and gray all at once. If I'd had a rifle, I'd have aimed it at her. I'm sorry for it now, but all I could think was that her pelt would make me more than a few dollars. I knew our machete hung on the wall to my right. I felt for it without turning my head and found its handle with my fingers. The she-wolf and I sized each other up a minute more. In the end, I didn't use the blade. She did me no harm and I let her pass without incident.

I thought about her for days. Wolf families travel together: mama, daddy and the young ones, even after they've grown. She was alone. If I believed in animal magic the way the Indians do, I'd say she was a spirit come to warn me. About what, I didn't know then, but I was sure that if she'd had a message to share, it wouldn't have been a good one. There was only sorrow in her look.

When I finally closed my eyes that night, I dreamed my wolf could talk. Her voice sounded unnatural: too deep for a woman's but not quite low as a man's, a raspy growl. She said I'd had all the happiness I was going to get in this life. She told me I'd see hell before Miles would come back to me. I woke up desperate to put my arms around him.

He was on his way to Oklahoma to take pictures of the dust that rose in amber clouds and suffocated the sun. I wished for him to come to me, seated on a galloping horse, riding a river's rapids in a tortoise shell, trailing on a string carried in an eagle's talons. I wanted to lay by the one I loved. Miles was half way across the country with only his camera for company, photographing Negro sharecroppers in Arkansas. He wrote to me about how they refused to quit the croppers' union even when the landowner put them out for it. They ended up rusted farm equipment discarded, living in a tent city on the side of the road.

Miles wrote to me that the Negroes had tarps and tent poles on hand, as if they'd always believed the roofs over their heads would fly away without warning. I pictured them crowded in tents among their things, with whatever wouldn't fit (chiffarobes, cast-iron bed frames) hanging around outside like laundry to dry. They made dinner around campfires that first night and gathered to sing hymns.

I asked Miles to tell me about the brave people he met in his travels and said I would try to be half as strong as them. Things didn't end well for the Negroes, but still I wished I could be half as brave and strong as them when it came to dealing with Rowler.

| ROWLER HIDING IN THE DARK |

Torch and I played Kris Kringlers for Christmas. It was a Hollow tradition where folks disguised themselves and went calling on kith and kin Christmas Day. People tried to guess who we were and, if our costumes were good enough, they'd never know. I wore a pair of Daddy's old coveralls with the pants legs rolled up and the inside stuffed with hay to give myself the look of a husky man. I pulled one of Mama's old stockings over my face and hair (I caught hell when she found it stretched full of runs, tucked behind the woolen socks in her unmentionables drawer) and a hat over my hair for good measure. Torch draped an old horse blanket over his shoulders and had me smear his face with soap and soot from a cold fire. He wore socks over his hands to hide their shape, which would have been a dead giveaway, and a scarf to cover the place where scars feathered against his neck.

We went straight to the McConville place. Geraldine answered the door and got to giggling so hard she near about peed her pants. Jenny dropped the pot of water she'd been holding when she saw us. She said we scared a year off her life. I think they might not have guessed who we were if I hadn't made a joke about Torch being the ghost of Christmas past. "What the hell is that?" Franklin asked from behind a white mule fog. "It's from a book," Geraldine said. "Bee done read it to me. Bee, that you?" Franklin pulled the stocking off my head and said, "Well I'll be damned. Who'd a' thought such a looker could go and make herself so homely?"

Torch emptied a bag of oranges he'd lifted from his daddy's store onto the table. One of them rolled off the table's edge but, even drunk, Franklin managed to catch it softly, like it was a glass globe. For all the fuss they made over those oranges, you'd have thought we brought them a load of jewels instead of some fruit.

I bought a box of Christmas crackers from Hiram at the store and somehow managed to keep them a secret from Torch, so when I pulled them out from inside my coveralls everyone was surprised. Geraldine squealed with every pop. Each of them had something different inside: a piece of candy, a joke printed on colored paper, a pencil. Everybody piled their prizes in front of Geraldine, and she shepherded them off to a hiding spot before we could change our minds and take them back.

Jenny served up soup for dinner with bits of meat in it from a squirrel Franklin caught in one of his traps. We stopped talking long enough to eat, then I helped Jenny clean up. Jenny brewed up some chicory and Franklin splashed everybody's cup (even little Geraldine's) with a finger or two of white mule. Torch told the story of baby Jesus and the star of Bethlehem. We sang Christmas carols in front of the fire until Geraldine dozed off and Torch said it was time for us to go.

On the walk home, I asked Torch to tell me about the summer he hopped trains all the way to Texas.

"Not again," he groaned.

"C'mon," I said. "When you tell it right, I feel like I'm there." Torch griped when I asked him to retell it, but I knew he loved to remember the first time he struck out on his own like a grown-up man.

"Well, it was the year I turned seventeen and I'd taken as much guff from daddy as I could stand for a while. And you. You were spending all your time with Silas Barnes back then. I sure was sick of the sight of you two with your lips locked together. So I jumped westbound freight cars and set out to make my fortune in the Texas oil fields."

We walked slowly so Torch could concentrate on telling his story and I could concentrate on listening to it. When I shivered from the cold, Torch threw his horse blanket over my shoulders.

"Don't forget to tell about riding suicide," I said.

"I reckon I'm the one telling this story," Torch said. "When I could, I'd find a dry corner in a boxcar and watch the countryside sail past the open doors. Every once in a while, I'd come across a train with a brakeman guarding the boxcars, or else they were all full up of mean, drunk hobos. One of 'em pulled a knife on me once. Those days I'd have to jump a coal bucket. They got nowhere to stretch out or sit proper. You got to hang on to the side and be careful not to fall asleep or the train wheels will make mincemeat out of you. That's what hobos call riding suicide."

"Did you ever see anybody fall?"

"You know I did."

"What did he look like after?"

"Like he got run through a giant threshing machine. Ask me about something else."

"Okay," I said. "Tell me about when they found the black gold."

"Fine. A few days after I got there, the Number Four rig hit pay dirt. This was east, not west Texas mind you. Most people thought we'd never strike oil, so when we did we drew a crowd like you've never seen. Cars were parked three deep. Hundreds of people shuffling around watching us work. Somebody even took to selling hamburgers for a dime apiece to the gawkers.

I was lucky I got there when I did, 'cause word traveled fast and in a few days' time, men were sleeping in packing crates next to the oil fields hoping for work."

I grabbed Torch's hand and said, "But not you. You already had a job and you worked your way into another one."

"Yep," he said. "I started as a roughneck, which is no kinda life. Roughnecks do all the dirty work nobody else wants to do. I finally convinced 'em to let me run the boilers. They didn't think I could do it 'cause of my hands, but I told 'em ..."

This was my favorite part and I'd heard it enough to say it along with him, so I chimed in: "I guess I know how to handle fire," I said, trying to sound like Torch. "Who else here's got the scars to prove it?"

"Why do you make me tell you this story if you know it by heart?"

"It's a good story."

"After a few weeks, the boss said I was the best boiler man he had. That was hot work, I'll tell you. And Texas is damned hot to start with. I needed some mountain breezes. So I came back, and here I am."

"And you got a letter from your Daddy?"

"Yeah. Told me if I came back we could run the store together -- regular business partners. You know how that turned out."

I knew that after Torch came home, Hiram didn't hold up his end of the deal. Torch couldn't change a thing in the store without giving Hiram fits. They had a two-day row over where they should stock a dozen sacks of Baker's Choice Flour.

We were at my front gate. Our weathered, gray house was almost invisible in the dark, so that our lit window seemed to float above the ground by some witch's enchantment.

Torch grabbed me by the arm and laid a big wet smack on my lips. I wasn't expecting it so I near about fell over backwards. I said what the sam hill did he think he was doing. I really just wanted a minute to pull myself together and get puckered up for the next kiss, but Torch said to forget about it and that it must have been the whiskey or the Christmas spirit that made him do it. I was downright vexed he didn't try harder to convince me to let him kiss me again. When the girls in books turn the boys down, it just makes the boys love them more. It stung a little when it didn't work for me. I told Torch it was good as forgotten if that's how he wanted it.

There was something else about that night with Torch. In the middle of all that kissing and arguing about kissing, I thought I saw something -- someone -- standing in the darkness at the tree line beyond our gate. I drank too much white mule at the McConvilles, so I chalked it up to that. I was still wondering about it later, so I looked out my window and saw a red eye set back in the woods. It fixed its gaze on our house. My first thought was that it was some kind of one-eyed hellhound come to collect me. I turned my lantern down so it wouldn't see me. The eye floated into the yard toward my window. Then I saw it wasn't an eye at all, but a lit cigarette. This was no demon. It was Rowler. The moon only half lit him up so he was hard to make out, but I'd have sworn on my life it was him. He dropped his cigarette and started walking toward the house. He got close enough to the front steps that I couldn't see him from my window anymore, even with my face pressed against the glass. I listened for the telltale scraping of the door knob's turn. Instead I heard a whistle coming up the path. Rowler went crashing through the yard. He turned tail and ran like the coward he was.

I couldn't pull away from the window until I saw what blessed thing had run Rowler off. A moment later he was there. Torch. I've heard it said too much goodness can send evil running. That night it was true. Torch sniffed the air and looked for trouble, my very own guard dog. Once he was satisfied everything was in order, he was gone. I never said anything about it to him. I was happy to know he was looking out for me. I didn't want to embarrass him by calling attention to it.

The next morning I found a burned up cigarette in the yard. It was store bought, not hand rolled like the ones around the Hollow. I only knew one man who bought his cigarettes in a box. I showed it to Mama. She said he must have left it behind the last time he visited, or maybe he came calling when we weren't home. I was so let down when she didn't believe me, I must have shown it. She told me to wipe the sick cow look off my face. She walked away when I started to cry.

| MORE FAMILIES GONE |

Ruth wanted a baby so bad, she wouldn't give up trying. Peter joked that practice made perfect, but once when Ruth left the room he said he wished she would let go of her dream for a child. "A couple times a year she's real sure she got herself a baby cooking in there," he spoke quietly so she wouldn't hear him from the kitchen. "When she finds out it didn't take she has one of her spells. I swear they done gone and gotten worse."

Most days, Ruth could light up the world. In the light, her yellow hair glowed like she was the sun or the moon one. When people saw that glow coming and her underneath it, they couldn't keep from smiling. But when she got her hopes up about a baby and then her womanly curse came, a mean melancholy hit her and strangled her mind for days. She weeped like Brontë's Catherine on the moors. She'd quiet down once there was no more water left in her to make tears. Then she would spend days asleep in the dark den of her bedroom. She ate nothing or swallowed the most unlikely foods mindlessly. I once watched her mix raw cornmeal with enough water to keep from choking, and eat the bowl empty with a wooden spoon. She stared straight ahead while she ate, like she was watching a good western at the picture show.

Peter exercised Job's patience with her. He held her a lot, but not like a lover. Back when Daddy had a few cows and one of them gave birth in a snowstorm, he brought the calf into the barn, undressed to the waist and held it to his naked chest to warm it. Peter held Ruth the same way. It didn't do much, except maybe lift her spirits an inch or two.

I used to bring her small presents. The rule I set for myself was that it had to be something I found on the walk to her house. I ended up with flowers in spring (yellow jonquils were her favorite). I brought berries in summer, colored leaves in the fall. In winter I had to get creative. Once,

I dug up a mole (no small task since they burrow deeper in cold) and brought it to her. It was a funny looking thing: pocket-sized with eyes so tiny I'd challenge anybody to try to find them, and spades for digging paws, spread wide as oriental fans. I made Ruth close her eyes before I put it in her cupped hands.

Another time I made a sort of stick sculpture out of twigs. It looked like two underfed people screwing. Ruth only stared at it until Peter, who was about as beefy as a skeleton, said, "I think I recognize my own ass." I'm proud to say we got a laugh out of Ruth on that one.

Folks didn't stop needing her medicine when Ruth was having a spell. Unless she was really bad off, she could usually muster the wherewithal to mix up her cure-alls. She wouldn't leave the house to deliver them, though. That's where I came in. Peter paid me thirty-five cents a day to deliver Ruth's remedies to the sickly folks who ordered them. If it were up to me I would have done it for free, but Mama never would have allowed it. She took the money from me as soon as I got home anyway, so Peter was really paying her to set me free for a few hours.

That January, I made five deliveries in one day. The first two were over in Corbin Hollow. I carried smoked jimson weed leaves to Eva Dallow for her asthma. My next delivery was Willie Hackett, who lived about two miles down mountain from Eva. His wife Mary sent for some bumbleweed tea to help stop his squirts. I followed the stench to the necessary house, where I found Willie moaning about his ass being on fire. The rest of the orders were for folks laid out with influenza. They got tea made from boiled buttonweed roots. I made sure to tell them to add a splash of fresh goat's or cow's milk. Ruth also sent along her famous fever plaster. She made it with flour, ginger root and pine sap to draw the heat out of the body. I relayed her instructions to the afflicted and their caretakers: heat the plaster in a bowl over a boiling pot of water, spread it on the chest and forehead and cover it with thin, cotton rags. Let it cool, then scrape it off and reheat it if the fever's stubborn enough to hang on through the first application.

I usually collected folks' money for the cures and delivered it to Ruth, or Peter if she'd taken to her room. In those days not too many folks had money, so most of them paid with whatever they had that was of value. It didn't make a bit of difference to Ruth, but it was awfully hard to hike to her house with the stuff folks gave me. I had to make it five miles back with two bottles of milk, half a dozen eggs and two old, good-for-nothing hens bound for the fryer.

Imagine my predicament when one of the hens wriggled free of my right arm and made a break for it. How do you catch a chicken with one arm without letting the bird under your other arm loose, while toting milk bottles heavy as boulders and a sack full of eggs that'll crack if you sneeze? I'll tell you -- you don't. Every time I picked one chicken up, I'd lose the other one. I finally figured out how to herd the loose chicken in the right direction until it was tired enough to let me pick it up without a fight. Then I'd let the other chicken wear itself out walking. I was never so happy to see the gate to Ruth and Peter's yard.

I about keeled over when Peter suggested I carry the chickens home to Mama -- another two miles. Oh how I cursed those birds. When Mama cooked them up, those hens were about as tasty as shoe leather. The toughness probably came from all that marching they did on their own poultry Trail of Tears. I prayed next time everybody would pay me in cornbread.

I'd been concentrating on the chickens during my rounds, but I had enough of my wits about me to notice the hollows were unnaturally still. I was used to hearing the sounds of living folks when I walked the woods. That day, half of the houses were empty shells with no life left in them -- forgotten spectral husks like the ones Miles described in his letters from the midwest, where dust storms forced people to move on from their memories. In the mountains, a whole lot of families had sold to the state and moved down to resettlement housing or off someplace else. Torch said families with money to spare like the DeKalbs bought level-land farms down in the valley.

You remember me writing about Ruth borrowing their car to take me for a spin? Well, when I passed by their place, I could have sworn I heard fiddle music coming from the house. They used to have the best shindigs. They had an upright piano, and I tell you little Rupert DeKalb could play the snot out of it. I followed my ears to the front of the house and peeked in the downstairs windows. There was no one there. The sound must have been a memory left over from when I danced at their last party. All the furniture was gone. There were lighter squares on the wood floor where rugs used to lay. When I turned to leave, I realized the window frames and their glass panes were gone too. Someone must have lifted them to use at their own place. My bet was on Red.

I have a confession to make. I had such a fierce need to escape the

Hollow that I would change Miles' stories, the ones he told in his letters, and put myself in them. I was such a silly girl. I never could believe he thought it was worth the postage to write to me.

We had a whole life together he didn't even know about. I imagined I was beside him in an Oklahoma dust storm. It was the two of us trapped in his car while the wind battered the windows and doors with dirt lifted from fallow fields. He undressed me gently and afterward told me stories about his travels until the wind let up. I was with him and a luckless family when they lost their baby girl and grandmother to pneumonia on the same day. I held his hand at the funeral after he took pictures of the girl and the old woman, sleeping in their side-by-side wooden boxes. I helped him and another man dig out a house when it was buried in dust up to the tops of its windows. In my mind's eye, it looked like we'd forced an earthen snake to spit out a kill too big for its unhinged jaws.

You might have figured out by now that I loved Miles as much for where he was bound than who he was. I'm sorry for it. He'd earned more than that from me. I can't excuse it except to say I don't think I knew it then. I do know if he'd asked me, I would have gone to him. I would have carried his camera bags, his film, his flashbulbs. I would have cooked for him over campfires at night, or helped the woman of the house if someone was kind enough to take us in. I would have made him forget the dust and the misfortune it delivered, if only for an hour or two in the dark, alone together. But he hadn't asked and I was beginning to wonder if he ever would. I had a desperate need to get away from Mama and Rowler in the worst way.

| CATCHING A COPPERHEAD |

I decided to go hunting for snakes that winter, when the prospect of earning a dollar made me itch like a trailing poison ivy vine had gotten a hold of me. It wouldn't do me any good to fix the still. Mama would tear down more stills than I could build. I figured I could catch snakes good as anybody. Buddy Collins paid a dollar a snake, but he only needed one or two every few weeks, so I wouldn't exactly make my fortune. It was easy work though. There were near about a hundred rattlers that hibernated in a den less than a mile from home. They used the same spot every winter, where the rock cropped out in the shape of an old man's face with one eye instead of two, a busted nose and battered cheekbones.

I took Daddy's snake stick with me. He carved it out of a hickory branch, so you could near about use it to ratchet a pick-up truck off its wheels without it breaking. One end of it was v-shaped -- perfect for pinning a snake's head. Daddy made the other end into a hook he used to lift snakes' bodies. I took Daddy's snake bag with me too. Daddy didn't have much luck with snakes in the end, but he never got a single snake bite when he was using his lucky stick and bag to catch them.

I had to dig the snow out around the den to get to the rattlers. Inside, each snake was coiled in its own corkscrew shape. They huddled together like a hundred rolled up pill bugs. There wasn't much fuss when they saw me. A rattle here and there, a few tried to slither away but the cold made them slow as molasses. A copperhead glowed pink on the edge of the group (the rattlers didn't mind since those pit vipers liked to stick together come winter). I went for her since I wasn't keen on grabbing for a snake in the middle of the pile. Her eyes had a new penny's bright flash. Her head seemed dipped in molten copper. The rest of her looked sun bleached -- four feet of rosy scales interrupted by faded black and brown cross bands.

Ruth had a butterfly in a glass box, its wings pinned to white cardboard backing. Peter gave it to her for one of their anniversaries. It was the most perfect monarch I'd ever seen: pumpkin orange rimmed by velvety black, spotted with enough white to make a hungry bird think twice. When I looked at it I always wondered at how someone managed to kill it with such care that its papery wings didn't tear. They must have sprayed it with poison. Poor butterfly, too pretty to live.

My snake was just as perfect a specimen, except nobody frames snakes for decoration. I didn't admire her for long. I had her in the bag quick as you could say dollar bill. I packed the snow back into place to keep the left-behind snakes warm. I was halfway to Mountaintop before I saw my hands were shaking. I guess the sight of a hundred vipers would make anybody nervous.

Buddy was so impressed with my copperhead I thought he might give me extra for her. I should have known better. He led me into the main house, then onto an enclosed back porch where he kept a rusty bathtub full of his show-stopping reptiles. We weren't in there more than a few seconds before a man's voice outside hollered, "Buddy Collins, get your ass out here you ugly old bastard" in that way men have of calling each other names to show their affection. Buddy told me to make sure I closed the top good, then he headed outside. I saw him through the window when he got out into the yard. He slapped the other man hard on the back. They locked hands and pumped their arms up and down with enough enthusiasm to coax water from a dry well.

I turned back to the task at hand. The tub was covered with a sheet of tin, weighted with cinderblocks. I could hear half a dozen snakes slithering inside, gripping the cool walls of the cast iron tub with their scales. I piled the cinderblocks on the floor and untied the bag that held my perfect specimen. I used Daddy's snake stick like a jack to lift the edge of the tin cover and tipped the opening at the top of my bag into the gap. I felt the weight of my copper-colored girl slide from the canvas into the tub. I put the tin back and went to collect my dollar from Buddy.

| THE MCCONVILLES VANISH |

Mama made me shoot a possum on the front porch before the sun got up one morning. She said he was vicious. He was hiding behind a planter when Mama got home from Buddy's. Apparently, he charged her and bared his needle-sharp teeth (the possum, not Buddy). Possums can be bad-tempered, nasty creatures. You'd think a member of such a species would have recognized Mama as a kindred spirit and let her be.

I took an old pistol of Daddy's onto the porch with me for show. I aimed to miss the pest and just scare him off. The damned fool animal charged me after I fired over his head, so I shot him. The first bullet just made him mad. He growled and hissed and came at me again. It took me two more bullets before I could get him to lay down and die. He was a three quart possum but I swear he sprayed six quarts of blood on the porch. It took me nearly an hour to clean up the mess.

After I finished wringing the blood out of the cleaning rags, Mama said she was feeling under the weather and sent me to tutor Jenny and Geraldine McConville by myself. I was looking forward to reading all of Geraldine's favorites (the ones Mama didn't think were suitable for us girls). I even had plans to introduce Jenny to something other than the drudgery of those old Dick and Jane readers. Torch saved me his daddy's Life Magazine from June. I figured Jenny could at least read some of the advertisements. But when I got there, the McConvilles were gone.

I don't mean they were out picking berries or shopping at MacArthur's. I could tell from the looks of their cabin they wouldn't be back anytime soon. The front door was wide open. Supper was on the table, only it looked like it had been served days before. The corn pone was gray with mold. The beans were cracked and dried in their bowls. None of it had been touched. People as poor as the McConvilles don't waste food. All of their belongings were still there. I checked the drawers of the only dresser they owned and I can tell you they must have left with nothing more than the clothes on their backs. Some of the chairs were turned over, slats broken, laying on top of logs pulled from the fireplace onto the middle of the floor, like somebody had tried to send the whole place up in smoke. Luckily, the logs had gone cold and turned to charcoal without catching the rest of the house on fire.

I stuck around long enough to clean up the food and set the chairs back. I bent to sweep the ashes from the floor. A corner of green paper caught my eye. I pulled it from the ashes. There was more to it. I could just make out part of a red circle and the letters L-U and S-T on top of each other. If the rest of it hadn't been burned, it would have said Lucky Strike. That meant Rowler had been there. Had his hands on Jenny. Geraldine too maybe. My stomach turned. I thought someone ought to kill that son of a bitch dead. The sooner the better.

I ran home to tell Mama about the McConvilles. She forgot she was feeling poorly and dragged me back to the cabin with her. It was downright ghostly the second time around. My efforts to tidy the place up made it seem like the family was just hidden in the loft's corn husks or under the blankets on the bed, waiting to jump out and say boo. But instead of a happy surprise, it stayed deathly quiet.

Mama ignored my evidence against Rowler. "That could be a page from a catalog," she said. "You know how Jenny's always cutting them up to decorate with."

I wished for a witness. Nobody lived within sight of the cabin, and the McConvilles had pretty much kept to themselves ever since they lost George, so there was no one we could ask about what happened to our friends. I knew they vanished at Rowler's hands. I would have staked my life on it.

After a time, Mama put her arms around me right there in the McConvilles cabin just as easy as if we were Jenny and Geraldine. "I know you're scared," she said. "We're going to be alright." I returned her pats on the back with one of my own. The rest of me stayed stiff. I wasn't surprised, mind you. Mama doled out comfort when I got low enough to lap it up like a starved kitten at a bowl of milk. I won't lie and say her measured love didn't sometimes lift the heavy millstone I carried on my back. But I hated to be beholden to her for the good in life since she was so quick to deliver the bad. And anyway, she threw Rowler in my face again a minute later, while she was still holding me.

"He'll save us," she said.

"No Mama. No."

| BUDDY'S SNAKE BIT AND FLAT BROKE |

Buddy paid me a dollar to dispatch him to hell -- at least, that's nearly what happened when the snake I sold him bit that son of a bitch in his sleep. Red found him on the ground outside his fancy stone house. Buddy must have tried to crawl to the guest cabins for help. He passed out naked in a pile of his own sick, which froze to his day-old whiskers in the February cold. Red said he didn't have the stomach to suck the poison out of Buddy's leg. The bite was so close to Buddy's man parts, Red would have felt the tickle of ball hair on his cheek if he'd tried. At least he had the sense to send his boy Bartholomew to Sperryville to fetch Doc Waters. He sent word to Mama and me through his second oldest, James. I guess Red had seen Mama hanging around with Buddy up at Mountaintop and figured she'd want to know.

When we got there, Buddy was laid out in his bed, still naked but with a sheet covering his personal places. His thigh swelled beyond what seemed possible. It flaunted a red, blue and purple rainbow of a bruise. Buddy's breath rattled in his chest. He was begging for water. His voice was small, weak as the rest of him, but no less desperate for it. Doc Waters injected him with permanganate of potash and tied a rag around his leg to keep the poison from traveling to his heart (although the poison had enough time to travel around the world and back before Doc even got there).

Mama started fussing over Buddy like he was kin. She punched the air back into his pillows, mopped his brow with a wet washcloth, held his head up so he could slurp from a cup of watery ice chips (Buddy'd had a Jamison walk-in freezer delivered to Mountaintop the year before. I never set foot in it, but the kids who did said if you kept a snowball in there it wouldn't melt in July). She stopped just short of singing him a lullaby. I don't know if she was trying to impress Doc Waters or Buddy with her sweet mothering, but her efforts were wasted on both of them. Doc Waters was hunched over his bag, packing up like his life depended on getting out of the Hollow before sundown. And Buddy, well, he kept calling the rest of us Jesus, Mary and Joseph. I was Joseph. Then, in between the holy names he'd yell, "Tits!" Mama pretended not to hear Buddy's cursing. Doc Waters patted Buddy on the shoulder and reminded him there were ladies present.

Before Doc said his goodbyes, Mama asked him for the bill. "I'll take care of Buddy's accounts while he recovers," she said. "I know he wouldn't want to leave a bill unpaid." Doc looked at Mama like she was delirious as Buddy and said, "Ma'am, Buddy Collins hasn't paid a bill in years. I treated him for consumption two years ago and he still owes me two dollars for it. I don't try to collect because I know he doesn't have a dime to his name."

Mama's eyes went wide. "That can't be true," Mama said. "I mean, I know he's had some hard times like everybody else, but you're saying he can't even pay a doctor's bill?"

"From what I've heard, he made some improvements to the resort about a year ago. Got everything on credit, then couldn't pay back the loans," Doc said. "It's my understanding his sister paid the notes to keep the family name in good standing."

Mama sat down hard in a cane chair by the bedroom door. I walked Doc Waters out. When I got back to the bedroom, Mama was still sitting. She looked stuck. I asked if she needed help getting up. She didn't seem to hear me. Then she told me to find the snake that got its fangs into Buddy and kill it.

I went to track down Red. He was the one who found Buddy, so I figured he'd taken care of the snake already. He was on one of the guest cottage rooftops patching holes. He hollered down, "He gonna live? That son of a bitch swore he'd trade me some blankets for fixing the roof and I ain't seen hide nor hair of 'em yet." Red's never been accused of being too sentimental. "'S gonna be a cold winter 'round my house if Sarah don't git some new blankets, and I ain't talking 'bout the weather."

Red told me he'd found the copperhead still curled up between Buddy's sheets, like it was her bed. He said he put her back in the bathtub with the rest of the snakes. He hocked a wad of tobacco juice off the roof, and the wind turned around and smacked him right in the cheek with it. He shouted "goddammit," before he wiped his face with his sleeve. Then he looked at the resulting brown stain on the arm of his coat and cursed again.

After the possum on the porch incident, I wasn't in the mood for any more killing. If I didn't do it, I knew Buddy would. Buddy was as spiteful as Red was ignorant. First thing he'd do when he got his wits about him would be to kill my copperhead. It shouldn't have made a bit of difference to me, but I decided to collect her just the same. I pulled her out of the tub with a stick I'd picked up outside and dropped her back into my snake bag, which I'd brought tucked into the waistband of my pants. After I put the tin sheet back on top of the tub, I was sure to stack the cinderblocks back on the corners. It occurred to me that I had forgotten to do that the last time I lifted the tub's tin ceiling.

I put my snake back where I'd found her. I tipped her out of the bag a little too close to my feet. She slithered over them on her way back to the poisonous pile of her sleeping friends. I near about peed my pants. I was still shuddering when I piled the snow back over the door to the vipers' Shangri-La. And that was the end of me and the snake business.

| BIG ROW WITH MAMA |

Rowler showed up at dawn, just down from Mountaintop I'd guess, smelling like he'd gone for a swim in a vat of white mule. Buddy usually cut the festivities off at the witching hour. Rowler and the guests must have been taking advantage of his convalescence.

I was in the barn. I milked Daisy first thing, then turned her out and cleaned her stall. Mama didn't usually come out, especially in winter, except when she needed cheering up. When she was in poor spirits, it lightened her mood to give me a hard time about something. That morning she was griping that the barn was a mess. I didn't have the tools hung on the wall the way she liked, so she took them down one by one and flung them into an angry pile in the middle of the aisle.

I noticed that the light from the open barn doors had gone dark before I saw Rowler. He took up more than a small portion of the doorway. His mustache wasn't twitching like the first time I saw him. It must have been worn out by the night's carousing. His eyes looked the same -- squeezed almost shut to keep folks from seeing in, gray like the color had leaked out of them.

He lit a cigarette a few feet from a stall floor covered in dry hay, then let the flaming match drop. Mama pretended to shift her feet, but I could see that she'd kicked enough dirt over the match to put it out. Every time he let another nugget of red ash fall, Mama smothered it the same way. She suggested they move outside the barn for their talk so they could enjoy the view (our back field dropped off at the end, so a person could see clear across the mountains). Rowler sucked air in through his cigarette, then breathed out smoke and said the view was just fine from where he was standing. I saw him look at me, so I turned my back. I took my time milking Daisy so I wouldn't have to meet his eyes.

He told Mama time was up. She'd better cough up the money for the resettlement house or find somewhere else to go. "Unless you've decided to take me up on my proposition," he said. I could feel him nod in my direction.

"I believe in working with authority, Mr. Rowler," Mama said. Her friendly tone gave me a jolt. I turned to face her too quickly and knocked over my milk bucket. I took the Lord's name in vain before Mama held up her hand to silence me. "But," she went on, "I'm only willing to enter into an arrangement that will provide for our future." She suggested they finish their conversation over coffee inside, and Rowler followed her to the house.

I hid under the porch until I saw his polished boots thump down the front steps. He stopped at the bottom. His left boot was a foot from my cheek and glossy as a looking glass. He could have seen my reflection in it if he'd looked down. Instead he walked away to wherever he'd parked his truck.

I busted into the house soon as he was out of sight. I asked Mama what the hell she'd promised him. I meant to sound hard, but my voice was thin and nervous as dragonfly wings.

"I don't know what you're up in arms about," she said. She kept washing the coffee pot to make sure I knew our conversation wasn't important enough for her to put it down. "You've got yourself a shot at a man with a government job. This day in age, plenty of girls would give their eye teeth for a man with money coming in. And a pension, too. All he wants is to court you."

"That's not true," came my flimsy, little girl voice. I willed it to be strong. "You know it's not."

"I know no such thing. You have a lively imagination Anabelle. That man may be a little rough around the edges, but he wouldn't hurt a fly. He cares about you. He told me so."

"He's lying and you're pretending to believe him to ease your guilt."

"He's willing to do right by you, which is more than I can say for that photographer you spend so much time writing to."

"Don't you talk about Miles." I was screaming, but somehow my voice still sounded small. "You don't know anything about him."

"Oh I know plenty, babydoll," she said. "My dearest Bee." She smiled.

She liked mocking me. She enjoyed letting me know I'd only imagined my letters from Miles had been private. "I fall asleep with your picture beside me. I wake up reaching for you."

I told her we were in love. I wouldn't expect her to know anything about it, I said, since she had to trick a man into marrying her.

"If he loves you so much, why doesn't he come back here and help us? He sounds more chicken than man to me. You'll latch on to Rowler if you know what's good for you."

I told her she was wrong. Tears came without my calling for them. I took off running. I ran through the woods with a child's recklessness. My feet hit the ground too hard. Branches reached out and scratched my face and arms. It was getting dark and everything was blurry to boot, on account of all my stupid little girl tears. I was aiming for Ruth's. I didn't realize I'd lost my way until it was too late. I was a stone's throw from the Outlaw Shep Jones' cabin and his dogs had raised the alarm.

I didn't have enough of a head start to outrun the dogs, so I hightailed it up a tree fast as a scared coon. Jones was known to have the meanest dogs in the Hollow. They used to say he didn't feed them, so they'd tear up and eat whatever living thing was dumb enough to set foot on his land.

To fully understand my predicament, I have to share another fact about Jones. He made it known he'd shoot anybody the dogs didn't get first. I knew as soon as I climbed that tree the dogs would circle the bottom and give me away to Jones, but I also knew shotgun spray would be a better way to die than to watch a half dozen savage beasts rip my arms and legs off.

Not a minute after the dogs spotted me, Jones and his two grown boys busted out of the cabin's front door onto the porch, Jones with a rifle and his two boys with a shotgun each. I expected them to call out, ask who goes there or some such thing. I guess they didn't give a good goddamn because they started in shooting right away. Shotgun pellets broke branches off all around me. I positioned myself behind the trunk of the big oak I'd chosen as my hiding spot. I could hear the tree splintering under fire. I knew if I didn't do something soon my number was up.

"Hey!" I hollered as loud as I could when they were reloading and I thought they might be able to hear me. "Hey! You sissies gonna shoot a girl?" This got their attention. All three of them came running.

"Hot damn. We done treed a girl," one of the younger ones said and laughed. "Can we keep her Pa?"

"Shut up." It was the Outlaw Jones in his black Homburg, eyes covered by its brim. I wondered if he slept in that hat. "We ought to kill you, girl, for coming 'round where you don't belong."

If I thought they'd take it easy on me for being a girl, I was wrong. I tried another tack I thought might sway the man called Outlaw.

"A government man ran me here," I said. "He was after my Mama to let him have me. I ran off to hide but I lost my way. I didn't mean no harm and I didn't see a thing I shouldn't have Mr. Jones. And if anybody asks me if I've been here, I'll have nothing to say about it."

Jones thought on this a minute. He lowered his gun. His sons kept theirs trained on me. Then, without a word, he turned to walk back toward the house.

I couldn't leave good enough alone. I had to know if he was part of the gang that robbed that train in Poplar Bluff. I called after him, "You from Missouri, Mister Jones?" As soon as I said it, I regretted it.

"What'd you say girl?" The grown-up boy who had laughed at me before said it. He looked mean.

Jones stopped cold, his back still to me. Oh how I wanted to see his face without that damnable hat. Torch saved all the wanted posters that came into the post office. We'd spread them out on the floor when we had nothing better to do and look for a likeness that could be Jones. If I just could have seen his eyes, maybe I would have recognized him. Not to rat him out, mind you. Just to know. I always hated a mystery hanging around.

"You Bee Livingston?" Jones knew my name. I couldn't believe he knew who I was. He turned his head just enough that I could see his profile. "Your Daddy gave my missus a ham once. I was clear 'cross Ragged Mountain when a squall hit. Damned if I couldn't get home for weeks. I reckon she and my boys would'a starved without it, and I reckon your family didn't have it to spare."

So here was Daddy -- come from beyond the grave to save me. "Yes sir," was all I could choke out.

"I figure I owe your Daddy one," he said. "But come around here again asking questions 'bout places like Missoura and I'll end your time on this earth. Make sure your mountain friends know anybody sets foot on my land, me and my boys shoot to kill." And then he walked away. His boys followed. When they got to the house, Jones whistled for the dogs to leave me be.

I made it the rest of the way to Ruth's house in a daze. I wanted to tell her all about the Outlaw Jones, but when I got there she was in the midst of one of her sad spells. I was still out of breath when I found her in the sitting room. I guess she didn't notice because she asked me to draw the curtains, then curled into a ball in a high back chair and closed her eyes. She stayed like that for a long time. I helped Peter mend fences for a while. I could tell Ruth's sadness had Peter weighed down like kittens in a sack of rocks, ready for drowning. He wasn't in a state of mind to fully appreciate the tale of my encounter with Jones, and he didn't have room on his back for my problems with Mama and Rowler, so I kept my mouth shut.

I went home after dark. I brought a quilt from my bed to the barn, where I slept with my books in the hayloft. Before I left the house, I stood by the stove to eat a piece of cornbread and down a glass of milk. Mama had nothing to say to me, nor I to her. She found words when I picked up a lantern to carry with me. She said she wasn't paying for fuel so I could daydream in a lit barn. I left without it. I found a box of wood matches on the barn floor. Rowler's. In the aisle, away from the hay, I lit one and read as many words of *The Great Gatsby* as I could before the flame blackened my fingertips. Then I lit another and did it again. I made it through a whole chapter that way.

When the matches ran out, I thought about the Outlaw Shep Jones. Something he said stuck out in my mind: Missoura. Folks on the mountain said Missour-ee. In fact, the only other person I ever heard say it that way was a traveling salesman, who hailed from St. Louis.

I thought about Mama, too. I wondered what it said about me that I could manage to breed hate in the one person who seemed required by nature's law to love me.

| DESTINED TO STARVE ON RESETTLEMENT ROAD |

I was happy to hear it when Miles finally set foot in sunny California. The folks he called Okies had let him document their travels with his camera, all the way to the shining coast. California must have confounded them. I wondered if the bountiful orchards, gaudy with plump, rosy fruits, were an offense. "Your people made a poor choice," they said. "If your great-grandfather had urged his horses past the flat grasslands on over the mountains, this could have been your land. Look at what this earth yields. Touch it. Then taste the grit in your mouths and remember your own dusty fields."

They were landowners turned field hands. They had homes in the middle west but spent their nights sleeping five or six to a car. California was a foreign country to them, with plants and animals they didn't recognize. I hoped their luck would turn. Until it did, Miles said they had resolved to rise every morning and take what the day brought them. Their hopefulness was a wonder to me.

There was change in the Hollow too. A number of families moved down to Resettlement Road. Torch took a day off from the store and we went down mountain to check it out.

The homes were nice enough, mostly wood frame with a few brick ones mixed in. They were two windows and a door across. They had windows on all sides, which was a dead giveaway they were designed by the government's people. Hollow folk were smart enough to know all that glass made it impossible to keep a home warm in winter. They were going to need a lot of firewood, but God knows where they were going to find it since the government clear cut the trees.

Torch and I walked ten houses deep on Dogwood Lane to call on the

Achesons. On the way, Torch told me that Grandpa Acheson's grandkids had to hoist his porch chair -- with him still in it -- into the back of a pick up and drive him down there, on account of he refused to stand up when it was time to go. He couldn't have been too hard to move since he hadn't eaten anything but field peas for seventy years. Folks said he was a hearty young man when he went off to fight the War Between the States, but he came back frail as a sickly sparrow and never recovered himself.

When we got to their new place, Grandpa Acheson's ass was still in that chair. Despite his delicate appearance, the old man had always been quick with a story or a bawdy joke, but we couldn't get a word out of him. He just sat in front of the fire and watched it burn. Every once in a while his eyes would check the fireplace mantel for the Colt Army Model 1860 revolver he'd taken off a dead Yankee officer back when he was young and had a need to fight. It had a wood handle, maybe oak. The killing part was mostly gray with a gold trigger. It was polished so clean it looked good as the day it was issued. I wondered if maybe Grandpa wanted to use it to shoot some more Yankees, namely the park rangers who were up mountain tromping around on his land.

"He's been that way since we done brought him down here," Sam, Grandpa Acheson's oldest grandson (who wasn't so young anymore himself), told us. He invited us to sit around the kitchen table out of Grandpa's earshot. "Nary a word in two months." He poured us each a quarter mason jar full of his latest batch of whisky. "First I thought he was mad at us. Now I think his mind's gone. His body's awake but his mind has just plumb gone down for a long night's sleep."

"None of the old folks are taking it well," Torch said and shook his head. "They found Emily Younger's grandma wandering around all the way up at the Reynolds' place in nothing but her knickers. She near about caught her death of a cold. I don't think the mercury hit thirty that day."

Both Torch and Sam had more to say. I didn't catch much of it because I was too busy letting my eyes wander around the inside of the house. It was bigger than your everyday hollow house. Its walls were straight and smooth, white as cotton scrubbed clean. The kitchen wasn't the simple stove with an old dresser used as storage and work space that I was used to seeing. It had a top and bottom row of cabinets built to match and screwed into the wall. There was a sink with water that came pouring out of the faucet, right into the house, soon as you asked it to. And there were no lanterns here. Light came from lamps plugged into electric outlets in the wall. Now I would have smacked any man who called me a hillbilly, and of course I'd seen running water and electricity in plenty of places, but to see these modest Hollow folk flip an electric switch in their own homes was a sight I was not accustomed to.

"How in hell do you pay for all this?" I blurted the question out with as much grace as an ox in a tulip bed. Mama said it was rude to ask people about sensitive subjects like money. I didn't see the point in talking if all you could do was exchange niceties.

Sam wrung his hands a little first, then said, "I wish I knew. We done paid our first electric bill with money I got for Hollow lumber. I got no trees to cut here. No orchard to bring in apple money. I sold some whiskey, but my best customers are down Luray way and I'm afraid if I get caught hauling white mule into town the government boys will come take our house away."

"I'll do it," Torch said. "I'll take your whiskey into town and sell it for you."

"Your mama'd be awful proud of you, boy," Sam said. Torch went quiet, as any mention of his mama would make him do. "She and your Daddy always saw to the neighbors. We Hollow folks take care of our own," Sam said. "I can't take you up on your offer, though. I'm the one's got to provide for my family."

"How many kids you got Sam?" I asked.

"Three still at home."

"That tiny garden plot I saw outside enough to feed all of them and you and the missus?"

"No," he said. "Not and have anything left to set up for winter. We been buying canned goods from MacArthur's Store since December. Got the house payment too. Never thought I'd have one of those."

I wish I could say Torch and I came up with a plan to help Sam, and all the other folks down in resettlement housing, make ends meet. I wanted to offer Sam solutions instead of just pointing out the bad. But for once, I had nothing to say.

| ROWLER STRIKES |

After a whole lot of trying, Rowler finally got a hold of me and did his best. I managed to get free and hide at Ruth's. She kept me, like her bottled babies, safe from fresh harm. Rowler had the law hunting for me in no time flat. He told everyone who'd listen I was a violent criminal or crazy or both. It started back at Mama's place.

I should have known something was brewing when Mama insisted we have supper before dark, then got antsy soon as we'd finished for me to take what was left of the day's milk to the spring house. It was cold enough to store it on the front porch, but she said if I left it out another possum was sure to come calling for it. She was in an unnatural hurry for me to get it done. Going against her when she had her mind set was never a good idea, so I picked up the pitcher and went on my way. She followed me as far as the doorway. She stood with the door wide open, wasting the warm inside air. Halfway to the spring house, it struck me that she was still watching. The strangeness of it slowed my steps. "Go on," she pressed. "Are you going to take all night?"

When I got there, I pulled the wooden door handle Daddy carved from a chestnut branch years before. Something made me stop. I looked back at Mama. I could have sworn I saw her Cheshire Cat grin floating in mid air. She swept in my direction with her hands to push me forward. I looked into the dark behind the half-open spring house door, frozen by a fear I couldn't explain. That's when a man's hand grabbed my own, with a strike quick as a snake's, and pulled me in.

Rowler tossed me like a rag doll into the shelves that held our perishables. A week's worth of eggs and butter came crashing down. Milk pitchers exploded. He pushed me down onto the trestle table where our potato bins sat. The pock-marked golden orbs went rolling. Then Rowler got to work. He tore open the shirt I was wearing. He pulled at my pants. A sound came from me that was more animal than human: the high squeal of a sparrow caught in a hawk's claws. I fought him. I thrashed and writhed. My flailing arms found a milk pitcher and brought it down on his head hard enough to send its clay shards raining over us both. The pitcher's milk must have mixed with Rowler's blood, because a trickle milky pink as dogwood blossoms ran from his forehead and chased after the broken pitcher pieces. Nothing I did could move him. He might as well have been one of the maharaja's elephants, moored to the Pequod's anchor.

I must have irritated him with the pitcher, because he took my head in his hands and bashed it on the table top. One time. Two times. Three times. His cheeks bloomed red from the strain of clobbering me. My sight went black around the edges. My hands traveled away from me, searching for another weapon. My right hand found the hilt of a corn shucking knife and punched its blade beneath Rowler's bottom rib before my mind could think to do it. The blade was short, but it went deep enough to make him suck in air. I lashed out a second time. I hit the arm he used as a shield with another sharp punch.

He rolled away from me and looked down at his wounds. I saw my chance and took it. I was through the door and into the woods fast as my feet would move. I could hear him panting, crashing through the trees behind me like a bear. He was coming fast, but no one could outrun me in the forest. In a pinch I could almost keep pace with a doe in the deep thickets, leaping and landing without snapping the downed branches underfoot.

I ran until the sound of Rowler's racket faded away. I'd lost him. I could have slowed but I didn't. I wanted to run fast enough to outrun what had happened. I wanted to run away from the truth -- that my own Mama had sold me to a man worse than the devil.

I came to rest at Ruth's when my used-up legs forced me to end my flight. I found Ruth and Peter in the barn, her sweeping by lantern light and him tending to a mule with a cracked hoof. They shepherded me into the house fast, like the mountain was watching, ready to report our movements to the other side. I must have been a sight: torn clothes, hair matted with blood, bite marks I didn't know I had until I saw them later in the wood-framed mirror on top of Ruth's chest of drawers. It took Ruth a few minutes to stop repeating the same words, "Poor Bee. Oh my poor Bee."

Peter brought some clothes down for me, then left me and Ruth alone in the kitchen where she cleaned me up and put salve on my wounds. She was just back from one of her spells. Her moves were more deliberate than usual when she was fresh from her sadness, like her body needed time to remember its hardiness. I appreciated the gentleness of her. She made me a cup of tea, then poured what was left of the hot water into a basin full of cold, with a few lye chips mixed in. The kettle must have weighed heavy in her hands because she used both of them to lift it. She dipped clean rags in the water, clouded with the soap, then wrung them out too weakly so that when she pressed them to my face, water ran down it in rivulets. When I was clean enough to satisfy her, she folded me into bed between wool blankets. I knew I'd lay awake all night, my mind busy figuring out my next move, but soon as Ruth turned down the lantern my eyes closed without my permission.

The next morning I helped Ruth with chores while Peter went down to MacArthur's to see if he could learn anything about what Rowler planned to do next. Soon as I finished, I made an excuse to Ruth and skulked around until I found a place where I could be alone. I ended up in the hayloft just like at home. As soon as I settled in, Peter came home and found me. When he dropped down onto the bale next to me he let go of a low, old man's grunt.

He said Rowler was making the rounds with a lawman, bad-mouthing me at MacArthur's and all around the Hollow. He was saying I attacked him like some crazy banshee for no reason. According to him, I started foaming at the mouth when he told me and Mama we'd have to leave our place before spring. He said I picked up a knife and came at him, screaming that he wouldn't live to see us kicked off our land. He told Peter he aimed to have me arrested and dragged off to the loony bin. At least I could say I hobbled him when I had the chance. Peter said Rowler was lurching in a way you could tell his wounds were worrying him with every step. There was a bulky bandage around his middle and his arm was in a sling.

Peter had more to say. "Ruth loves you like her own kin," he said, "so do I. I ain't got no way of knowing if this'll blow over, but you'll stay with us until we get it good and figured it out." Then Peter got all sober and solemn. "It's the death of Ruth we lose you, Bee. You got to promise me you'll lay low. Rowler's won the law over to his side. They'll be crawling all over the Hollow looking for you. It wouldn't surprise me if they hid somebody in the woods who could watch folks -- my grandaddy said that's how they found deserters during the War Between the States. You can't set foot outside during the day, not even to the necessary house. Best to stay inside come nightfall too."

I promised Peter I'd do what he asked. I was in a real fix. I had to get to work on figuring my way out of it. I just needed a day or two to get my thoughts together. Meantime, I knew I'd be safe with Ruth and Peter.

| HIDDEN |

I wasn't meant to spend entire days indoors. It felt unnatural. I figured that out halfway through the first day of my internment. I knew Ruth and Peter wanted to keep me safe, but I was starting to think I'd have been better off stabbing myself instead of Rowler. My skin felt itchy, like when I was a little girl and Mama dressed me in clothes her rich city cousins sent along. The difference was I could shed those dresses. If I even cracked the door to get a good whiff of outside air in my nose, Peter shooed me back into the house.

I took over some of the household chores to keep myself busy. I tried to do the wash, but Peter wouldn't let me walk the dozen steps to the creek for water. We finally worked out a system where he left buckets full of clean water on the side porch. Ruth brought them in for me, then took my used pails into the yard where she tipped out their dirty water. When I was finished with the clothes, I hung them in the front room to dry. I tried my hand at cooking. Mama liked to do most of the cooking at home, so I wasn't very good at it. I fried a chicken black on the outside but it was so raw when we cut into it I swear it could have walked right off the table. Ruth tried teaching me how to knit, but the stocking cap I turned out looked more like a sock. I just wasn't comfortable working with a roof over my head.

The first night, I walked the house in my socks so I wouldn't disturb Ruth and Peter's sleep. All that indoor air made sleep unnecessary. I wasn't hungry either. Food tasted the same, no matter if it was sausage or beans.

I didn't have my books with me, but Ruth and Peter had five to choose from. Of course, that was including two copies of the King James Bible so they really only had three books I was interested in. They had a book called Flora and Fauna of the Blue Ridge that Doc Waters' Missus gave to Peter when he was a boy laid up with the mumps. Peter must have liked the book, because when he was grown he bought himself the second one in the series, called Flora and Fauna of the Blue Ridge II. Come to think of it, they really just had one book that interested me. It was about famous artists of the nineteenth century. Buddy gave it to Ruth as payment for some medicine she cooked up to help him with a cough. Some of the pages were dog-eared. Somebody's name was written by hand inside the front cover, Edith Watson. My guess is she was a Mountaintop guest who forgot to pack it in her back-to-the-city suitcase. The book's pages were glossy with every color ever invented. My favorite picture was of a painting by a man called Monet: Fisherman's Cottage on the Cliffs of somewhere I can't remember. It looked like a house you might see in the Hollow, except there was an ocean behind it instead of our mountain's rise.

I had the idea of reading to Ruth and Peter after supper. They mostly liked to hear stories from the Bible, which weren't my favorite. I did enjoy the psalms more when I thought of them as poems. When it was late and I wanted a drink, I read the commandments. Both Ruth and Peter would be snoring by thou shalt not steal. I used the opportunity to sneak into the cabinet where Peter kept the good liquor and take a swig or two, since Ruth frowned on my drinking during the day. Sometimes I put a blanket over them. I liked to study them in their sleep. Ruth's head always found its way to Peter's shoulder. His shoulder seemed proud to bear its weight. Internment or no, I was glad to be with them. Two better people I have never known.

Some nights I sneaked outside, but for that I'd wait until they were on the other side of their bedroom door. The first few nights I went outside in just the nightgown Ruth lent me, arms and legs bared to the cold. I was so happy to be free I hardly felt a chill, even though I could see my own breath. Then I remembered what Peter said about spies in the woods, so the fourth night I put on pants and a coat and carried his hunting rifle with me. I wore two pairs of socks to warm my feet but went without shoes, so my steps would be hushed. I stalked the woods around the house until the sky hinted at sunrise. I half expected to come across Rowler, lying in wait, ready to pounce on me. The thought of it made my stomach churn. But the idea of him watching me in secret, biding his time until he was good and ready to come for me, bothered me more. In the end, all I rustled up was a hoot owl, cross because I came between him and his mouse supper.

On the fifth night, I got hit with the urge to see Mama. Not because I wanted to cry on her shoulder or some other such business. No, I wanted to rub her nose in the fact that I'd been right about Rowler. She knew damn well Rowler was waiting for me in the spring house when she sent me. I knew that. But I also thought I knew that, much as she could get her back up over me, she didn't mean for me to get abused the way Rowler intended. She'd been taken in by him. His government paycheck confused her judgement. The bruises he'd given me still hung around my neck clear as day, my own strand of proof. There'd be no more denying his nature. I would make her see it my way.

Even though it was a sight past midnight, I wasn't fool enough to barge in the front door. That would have been a good way to get spotted by Rowler, who good sense said might be watching the place. I came up to the back of the house. I didn't dare set foot in the clearing around it. I stayed in the dark against a thick pine. It hit me that someone else might be doing the same, and that I wouldn't know about him until I made a move and he came after me. I picked up a rock and chucked it to one side. Nothing. I chucked a few more. No movement answered. I ran for Mama and Daddy's window, had it open and slipped my whole self inside quick as a long-tailed weasel after a rabbit.

Mama's bed was empty. Her voice came under the closed door to meet me, hateful and low. "Everything you touch turns to shit," she said. She was in the next room, working her rocker. I was fixed to answer her when a man's voice came back.

"How you figure this is my fault?" It was that bastard Buddy Collins.

"It was your idea for me to throw my own child to the wolves," Mama said. "I said I'd make her go off with him. You just couldn't wait, could you? Had to have him jump her in the dark. He's liable to have killed her. My daughter, my husband. What did you ever give up?"

"You never gave up one goddamned thing you didn't want to lose. You're the one sent her out there to meet him or are you going to blame me for that too? He was never going to kill her. He's got enough trouble around here without a dead body on his hands. The only one's done any killing is me. That was your idea, or did you forget? Lot of good it did us."

"I had no way of knowing that stupid hillbilly stopped paying on the life insurance I got him," Mama said. "He told me he was keeping up with it. If he had, we wouldn't be in this mess. But you. You lied to me and said you wanted the money to grow Mountaintop -- make it the biggest resort in the east. People would come from as far as New York, you said. But you needed that money to dig you out of the hole you were in. What kind of a man lets his sister cover his debts?"

"I wonder if there's ever been a woman in the history of the world so put upon as you. How is it you come out of all this lily white?" Buddy kept on talking but I couldn't hear him on account of there was such a loud buzzing inside my head. Daddy. What had they said about Daddy? Buddy picked those snakes on purpose. And the idea came from Mama, to kill her own husband?

The room floated away from me or me from it, I couldn't tell which. I managed to make it through the window again. On the other side, I felt underwater. You know that feeling when you go under? Everything's muffled and wavy and you can only move fast as whatever pool you're in will let you. If Rowler'd been there, he would have caught me and I wouldn't have given a damn.

I spent the first half of that night getting my head straight, and the second half working out how I was going to kill Mama. Most every way I came up with to get it done was too good for her. Shooting was too quick. So was choking her with my own two hands. Hanging was better. At least that way she might soil herself and have to meet Lucifer stinking to high heaven of shit. My favorite one to think on was catching her in a bear trap. A peace came over me when I pictured Mama bleeding, her leg bone snapped between the trap's metal teeth.

| IMPRISONED AT THE COLONY |

Before I could kill Mama, near about everything I loved in the world was gone. The destroyer was me. I should have gone with Rowler when Mama asked. I thought I was too good to be with a man I didn't want. I could claim I didn't know what would come, but didn't I? Stupid girl. Did I think Ruth and Peter could hide me away forever -- secret mother and father to their own cherished doll?

Rowler and his man came at dawn. Ruth shuffled me into the lost babies' pantry as soon as she heard their boots hit the porch. From my hiding place, I could hear them kick the front door open. Then came a stomping and clattering that sounded like a herd of goats had the run of the house. Peter argued with them. He said they had no right to barge into a man's home uninvited. Rowler told him to shut up. I stood still, quiet as those babies in their jars. He demanded to know where I was. When Peter didn't answer, Rowler forced some friendliness into his tone, but his words still came out rough as dried corn on the grinding stone. "Now listen here, friend," he said. "Man to man, this girl is more trouble than she's worth. And she's about to bring a whole world of hurt raining down on you if you don't cough her up. Her mother says the girl is friends with your wife. We know she's here."

Ruth denied it. She said I'd only stopped over for a night, then headed on to Richmond where Mama had people. Peter said they'd given me a few dollars, some clothes, and a ride as far as Waynesboro. Someone was pacing. The sharp urgency of the steps made me think it must be Rowler. Ruth and Peter kept on with their story. Ruth said I promised to write her when I got settled. She'd be happy to let Rowler know when she got word. They were law-abiding folks, Peter said. They didn't want any trouble.

That's when the pacing stopped. The steps came slowly and with purpose toward the door to my hiding place. For the first time, I looked down and saw that the light from the windows behind me shone under the crack at the bottom of the pantry door, except for a thick place in the middle, where my body cast its shadow. Had Rowler seen the same thing? He was coming. Two steps, three: the number of times he brought my head down on the spring house table. His feet stopped outside the door. I turned to escape through the window, but my way was barred by Ruth's shelves. I didn't have it in me to pull them down and see the babies' glass wombs explode at my feet, so I waited. I held my breath for what seemed like a long time but probably wasn't. Then the words came, "She's in there. Get her out." More steps. A long, lean lawman with a skunk's white shock of hair at his left temple opened the door and had me before I could run.

The lawman wrapped his arms around my waist and dragged me into the yard. Ruth pulled at me, but her frail tugs wouldn't have freed a fly from a spider's gossamer web. She screamed for Peter. He was already there, on the other side of me, pulling too. Peter punched the lawman in the back harder than I would have thought a man with his slight frame could. The arms that had me loosened. I took a step toward freedom. Then came the shot.

What happened next still runs through my mind from time to time, like a projector's in my head playing a moving picture on the back wall of my brain. It doesn't do any good to close my eyes, that just makes the pictures brighter.

The lawman, Peter, Ruth and I fell to the ground. Rowler was the only one left standing. He slid his gun back under his belt and wiped his hands with a white kerchief. The lawman got up right away, not a scratch on him. My eyes found Ruth next. She wasn't hurt. She lurched toward Peter. He was on his back in the snow. An exotic flower bloomed red from his gut, spreading its petals wide on the icy white snow behind him.

I felt the lawman's hands on me again, but Rowler said, "Leave her. She's not going anywhere." He motioned for the lawman to go back into the house with him.

Ruth was hunched over Peter. I thought I heard him whisper to her. It might have been the sound of his last breath leaving him, but I believe it was a last testament of love. Ruth howled. I'm not sure if I saw her leave me, or if she was already gone. When I got to her, I squeezed her hard like

I'd seen Peter do but it was no use. That familiar sadness had laid claim to her again, with a violence I hadn't seen before. Her heart still beat her alive, but there was no living soul in her eyes.

That night we were together, her and me, at the Virginia State Colony for the Epileptic and Feebleminded. It was hell by another name. A sneering nurse welcomed us before two beefy orderlies tossed us -- "hillbilly garbage," they called us -- into a locked room. We didn't get to leave that room more than once the first week and that was just for a lecture from the head nurse (the sneering one) about what she called personal hygiene and lady-like behavior. "I know this is new for you mountain people," she said, "but you've got to learn to live less like animals." She said we'd be allowed more freedom once she could be sure the wildness had gone out of us. Meals were delivered to our room twice a day -- always the same gray gruel. We relieved ourselves into a pot that was emptied once a day. A bucket of cold water and a bar of soap appeared at the end of the week, no towels.

Ruth wouldn't feed or bathe herself. I managed to spoon feed her enough that she wouldn't starve, but I couldn't get her to take more than that. I washed her, then dried her skin with the woolen blanket from my bed. If I didn't dress her she would have stayed stark naked until she was sure to freeze or come down with pneumonia or both. I told the Colony folks she was mourning her dead husband. I was afraid if she didn't come back to me soon they'd think she really was around the bend and never let her out of the place.

Even in sleep there was no escape from the moving pictures of that last day. They played nightly in my dreams. I would see Rowler and the lawman carrying Ruth and Peter's life, piece-by-piece, into the snow: the kitchen table where Ruth mixed her potions; the bed where she and Peter laid in each other's arms every night; Ruth's Limoges china, the set with the trailing pink roses that her mama left her, snapped into splinters on the ground. I saw Rowler holding a can of kerosene, then Ruth's house on fire -- lapped up by orange flames, their brilliant blaze vulgar against the somber snow.

I knew there was the sound of Ruth's screams. Every time the house popped and sizzled, the animals in the barn bayed. Rowler hollered at the lawman to arrest us. But the only sound I heard in my dreams was the gentle, wet rustle of the snowfall, which became a roaring in my memory.

| SALVATION IN A SUNFLOWER |

The smell of ammonia was everywhere at the Colony, sharp as skunk spray. It was more entity than smell. It stalked the halls in its dogged search for yet another set of nostrils to scald. I thought I would never smell anything else. The chemical was one prong in the goddamned nurses' all-out war on the natural world. They chased all the color away. Walls, floors, furniture, bed sheets -- even the clothes they issued us -- all were gray. And since we didn't get any natural light, I swear the pink faces of the patients (that's what they called us) had turned the white-gray of egret feathers. The windows were to remain closed at all times. God forbid a cool breeze blow through and send us into a tizzy. And if they caught you trying to gaze out a window at something to do with nature, they'd slam the blinds shut so fast your head would spin.

The chicken-shit nurse with the sneer was the boss. If I could think of something worse to call her I would. Maggot-eaten, deer innards? A still-steaming pile of dog shit? She was a grisly bitch, that one. The other nurses seemed to think we were there for our own good, so the worst I can say about them is they were idiots. But Chicken Shit -- I'll call her Chick -- she made it her mission to break good people into pieces. There were crazies there to be sure (I once heard the orderlies laughing about a woman patient they caught drinking her own piss straight from her necessary pot). Chick ignored them. She seemed most interested in us Hollow folk. There were a dozen of us that I knew about. We were never allowed to walk the halls or sit in the common room, so I didn't lay eyes on most of them. But I matched half a dozen voices to my neighbors with my ear to my door. The rest I couldn't place, but I knew. Hollow folk had an easy way of talking, sort of slack like they were saving their energy for something more important. I could have picked one of their whispers out of a crowd.

I wondered what they were in for. If they'd fought like me, I hadn't heard about it. Everybody left in the Hollow was bound to have heard about me and Rowler a day or two later. News of hair-raising happenings spread like a pox since most days were plain. I figured they must have done something wrong to have gotten locked up in that hell hole.

At least Ruth was allowed to wander a little. Chick didn't mind her. It was me she hated. I told Ruth if I had a chance, "I'd tell Chick to come on, sister. Five minutes alone with her and I'd rip her limb from tree." Of course, I was all talk. And anyway, Chick was no fool. She always had at least one orderly at her elbow. One afternoon she showed up with one of her thugs to deliver one set each of gray patient suits for me and Ruth to wear. For two weeks, we'd been wearing the same clothes we'd had on our backs when we got there. We washed them in our bath water and hung them to dry while we slept. Ruth hadn't been feeling herself, some bad flu or something. I helped her put her patient suit on first, so that when Chick came back I was still in my Hollow clothes. She sent the orderly for a pair of scissors, then had him hold me down while she cut them off of me. She threw me into an empty room alone with just my underclothes for cover. There wasn't a stick of furniture, not even a piss pot. I held it in for a long time, but nobody can keep from peeing for two days. When I finally let go, I used a corner of the room to keep it out of the way, but a thin yellow stream rolled between my legs and pooled in the room's middle.

There were two windows in my lonely room. One was a transom over the door to the hall. The other was to the outside, but it was high up, close to the ceiling, where I couldn't reach it to see out. It didn't take me long to figure out how to shimmy up a floor-to-ceiling pipe that ran near it so that I could get a look outside now and then. The window was open but striped with black bars that only a field mouse could squeeze between. The first time I looked through it, I saw a Negro man about a quarter acre yonder who looked dressed as a sunflower. His pants were green as a stalk, his shirt the yellow of petals. He turned his brown face up toward the sun. Even at that distance I could see he was all goodness. He hoed alongside a woman and a girl who wore gray patient suits. He'd give them gentle instructions every once in a while, then he'd pat one or both of them on their backs and go right back to work himself. All three of them brought hoes to bear on stubborn dirt clods. Once or twice they raised and lowered them with the unity of a chain gang.

After I watched the Negro man that first day, I experienced my own welcome miracle. For the first time in a month, I saw something in my mind's eye other than Ruth and Peter's house burning. I saw sunflowers.

| PRETENDING TO BE A LADY |

It helped me to have my floating window and a breath of outside air every once in a while, but I didn't like being in that room away from Ruth. I spent my days hanging from the tall pipe, looking out. I'd climb down to rest once my body started to shake from the effort of it. Sometimes the welcome smell of pines mixed with musty earth would sink with me to the floor, clinging to the strands of my hair.

I could tell the moment spring landed. My desperation to put my feet in living earth got so intense I would have chewed one of my legs off if it would have freed me from my trap. I got it in my mind that if I could get outside for a few hours a day I might survive the Colony. The only way I could see to do that was to get myself assigned to that sunflower-dressed, Negro man's work crew. It occurred to me that all I needed to do was make myself into someone who pleased her, and Chick might just go along. I swayed her to my side fast. I even figured out how to bring Ruth along. I'll tell you how I did it.

That nurse was pretty easy to figure out. She was always talking about minding one's manners and what was proper and what wasn't. So I stood up straight every time she walked into the room to see if she'd notice. I answered her questions with yes ma'ams and no ma'ams. Next thing I knew she had the orderlies bring some clothes, a bed and a piss pot into my room, along with a pail and mop so that I could clean up my filth. She even let me fetch my old bedclothes from Ruth's room.

Once the bed had been delivered, Chick told me I was welcome to sit in her presence. I sat down delicately on the mattress, like it was a fresh egg, and crossed my legs at the ankles like Mama taught me. The way that nurse looked twice at me, you'd have thought butterflies were coming out of my ass. Later I got word that she was going to let me eat lunch with everyone else. I tore a corner from one of my bedsheets and tucked it into the waistband of my patient's pants. I had a plan for that blessed little square of fabric.

There was no gruel in the dining hall. I walked down the chow line and watched my tray fill with the best food I'd seen since I'd been locked up: meat in a brown gravy, green beans and apple sauce. The green beans tasted like meat and the meat a little like applesauce, but it didn't matter to me. I'd noticed sharp points on my body where there had been roundness before, but I didn't know how starved I was until the smell of roasted meat hit my nostrils and my hunger overtook my good sense. It was all I could do not to drop my face to the food and eat it like a pack mule with a strapped-on feed sack. But I didn't dare sabotage all the effort I'd put into winning over Chick. She was circling the room, stopping now and then to rap some poor soul across the knuckles for slurping their coffee or holding their fork with the wrong hand. I ate with my fork in the proper hand when I knew she could see me, but those flimsy prongs were a poor delivery system. Every time I speared a piece of meat or scooped a few beans, most of the watery bite would run between the tines back onto the plate. I don't think I need to tell you I didn't have any more luck eating the applesauce. I finally gave up and scooped the food into my mouth with my fingers when that nasty nurse wasn't looking my way.

By the time she made it to my table, I had cleaned my tray. I felt her behind me. I pretended not to know she was there. It was time to put that little fabric square to work for me. I faked a sneeze, sniffing and snuffling until I achooed right into my makeshift handkerchief -- and not my usual hearty sneeze, either. No, this was a girly squeak punctuated by a fluttering hanky. I'll show you butterflies, I thought. Right then and there Chick said to one of her orderlies, "We might turn this one into a lady yet."

She called me to her office that afternoon, asked me if I had plans for myself. I told her I aimed to be an upstanding member of society. I'd like to marry a civilized man, I said, give him a child or two, keep house and tend to my family's garden (actually, I remember thinking I would have much rather traveled the country with Miles and his camera but I knew the truth wouldn't score me any points with Chick). "I know I've got a lot to learn," I said. "The way we keep house in the Hollow isn't up to in-town standards. And I grew up surrounded by good-for-nothing folks too lazy to keep a patch of weeds, much less a nice garden. I've been watching you, trying to learn how to be a lady. I don't know how I'll figure out the rest of it."

She sat up a little straighter in her chair when I mentioned using her as my guide. That was when I knew I'd caught my fish. Now I just had to keep her on the line until I could get her into my bucket.

"Oh you'll never convince a city man to marry you, sweetheart," she said. "But I'll bet you could land a nice country fellow -- a farmer of some kind." She rubbed her nose while she thought it over for a minute. When she was satisfied that she had the right plan for me, she said with some excitement, "Yes, with a little help from me you could make a good wife to a farmer."

We started with cleaning lessons. She had me tidy her office, which had already been scrubbed shiny (my own face stared back at me from her desktop). The only thing I saw out of place was a teaspoon, its soupy contents leaked onto a dainty, cream-colored saucer with a silver rim. She wiped the saucer clean with her own crocheted handkerchief before her tea cooled.

For a whole hour one evening, I pretended to soak up every bit of housekeeping advice Chick doled out. That was when I noticed her left hand kept getting away from her. It flew away from her body like a bird, so that she had to catch it with her other hand and hold it down. I'd seen her hands tremble a bit before, but I'd always assumed it was because she was worked up over something a patient had done. Now it looked like she had the same palsy I'd seen Ruth treat Old Man Spinks for more than once.

When she saw that my eyes were following her fluttering hand, she got short with me. "You listening to what I'm telling you?" she asked. "Bleach is every good housekeeper's best friend, but use it the wrong way and it can ruin a good shirt. You'd do well to pay attention to what I'm teaching you."

"Yes ma'am," I said. I asked her a few questions about bleach to make my next question less suspicious. Then I said, "When will you send me out to work in the gardens?"

"Outside?" She shook her head slowly, deliberately, like she was afraid it might try to fly off with her bird hand if she gave it too much rein. "Oh no, you won't be going outdoors. I can teach you everything you need to know right here inside these four walls."

"But won't I need to know how to keep a proper garden if I'm to be a farmer's wife?"

"Outside work is for men. Anyway, if your farmer needs help I guess he can teach you. Either that or you can give him a few sons who can help him bring in the crops."

I knew I shouldn't press her on it, but I did. I had a need to be out in nature like I had a need to breathe air and drink water. She got aggravated and it was off to my room for me.

She sent for me the next evening after she was done with her nurse duties. She had laid out what must have been three pounds of silver she brought from home, just as shiny as the desk it now adorned, alongside a neatly-folded pile of bright white rags (a job well done by her beloved bleach) and a pot of thick, gray polish cream which had been carefully molded into the smooth slope of a bowl's inside to erase the pits left behind by the hard-working rags. She explained that, while she highly doubted I would ever own anything of such remarkable quality, silver polishing was still an important part of my housekeeping education. I didn't see the use in keeping forks and spoons that required more tending to than an orphaned newborn calf, but I didn't tell her that. The calf would eventually give you back milk or meat, which is more than I could say for those pieces of metal.

It was late when I finished with the silver, and I could see her hand was trying to fly away again. She said I'd best be off to my room since she needed to get home. She had no ring on her finger, so I guessed there was nobody waiting for her there except maybe a few cats.

I motioned toward her loose hand and took a chance. I said, "Ruth cured Old Man Spinks' palsy. She could chase yours away too." I was lying. Ruth had told me a long time before that nothing could cure palsy. Best thing to be done was to build a man's strength with a good spring tonic and hope his body could calm itself.

Calling it out like I did must have embarrassed her hand, because it went and hid itself under the weight of her thigh. Chick looked straight at me but stayed quiet, like she was measuring me for the wooden box I was going to need when she was through with me. I kept talking anyway. I told her Ruth knew how to cook up medicine more powerful than anything city doctors could get ahold of. "Course, she'd need the ingredients," I said. "I'm sure she could find everything she needs on the grounds here.

A few trips outside ought to do."

"Your friend Ruth has been sick every day since the two of you got here. She vomited on an orderly's shoes today. She's in no condition to go wandering around looking for herbs," she said. "How's she going to make medicine?"

"I'll help her. We can probably find something out there to fix her stomach right up too. Send me along with her and I'll help her round up the right cuttings. She can tell me what to do and I'll mix up the medicine myself."

"Go to your room," she said. Her voice was flat. "If you know what's good for you, you won't mention this to another soul."

I thought my goose was cooked. I hardly slept that night. Every time I closed my eyes I saw Ruth sick and alone in this place. I had to get to her. Had to get us both outside to breathe real air. That would fix her. But I was sure Nurse Chick would see to it the only way Ruth and I left that place would be on our backs, dead as doornails. Behind my eyelids, I saw a vision of us dead in our gray patient suits. Turns out all that worrying was wasted energy, because an orderly came by the next morning and told me in a few hours he'd be back to gather me and Ruth up for "outside detail."

At first I thought it would be enough to feel the sun on my skin. Then I realized Ruth and I had to make a break for it. I was sure if I could get her back to the Hollow, I could find some of her kin to hide her until all the trouble blew over. I had done this to her. I had to find a way to fix it.

| WORKING FOR MR. SUNFLOWER |

Mr. Sunflower's real name was Alfred. He worked hard at trying to convince me and Ruth he was stone-hearted, but I knew better. I'd seen his gentleness, big as a bonfire, all the way from my window across the field. He could pile dirt on those tall flames all day if he wanted. They wouldn't smother so easily. The truth was I didn't believe it was us he was in a temper over. I was pretty sure it was the orderly tailing us every day who had Alfred's nose out of whack. Nurse Chick charged the most beastly of her thugs with tracking us like he was a hound and we were rabbits. The first week, he stood so close his shadow hung over the rows we hoed. One morning after a hard rain, the pants of his gray orderly suit got spotted brown with mud flung in his direction (not altogether accidentally) by our swinging garden tools. After that, he stopped well before the edge of the turned dirt, where he could keep his feet in the clean grass.

Once Nurse Chick's man couldn't hear what we were saying, Alfred would grumble at us. "Never had no damned orderly hanging around. 'S like they don't trust a man to do his job." Then he smoothed the tight curls on top of his head with his hand. He did that a lot. "How much trouble you two cause they can't let you outta their sight?"

Something else Alfred did a lot was badmouth his own self when he was talking to the orderly. When the orderly tried to take us back too early one evening (a good half hour before the usual time), Alfred pointed out his mistake. Irritation screwed up the orderly's face like an oncoming sneeze. Alfred saw it and offered up a quick apology, even though he was right. "Don't pay me no mind, sir," he said. "I'm just a lowly colored, no good to nobody 'less I'm swinging a hoe."

Seemed to me like Alfred should have been the more respected of the two men. His work fed everyone at the Colony. He didn't spend his time mopping up other people's messes and generally tending to Nurse Chick's dirty work. The way Alfred talked I guess he thought differently. And the orderly, he wore his white skin like it was a medal he'd earned. He was tall but scrawny as a scarecrow. He might as well have been a chipmunk with as much food as he stored in his pockets. He pulled out a new scrap every few minutes -- a chicken leg or a cheese wedge -- and ate it behind his hand like he was hiding something. All that eating and none of it stuck to him. I'd hate to see what would've happened if he hadn't carried a picnic lunch in his pants. I expect he'd have shriveled up and blown away in no time.

It would have taken two of that scrawny orderly to make one Alfred. Alfred's body was solid as a tree trunk, and he had a face that looked carved from one, but with a small axe instead of a knife, or some other kind of tool that made deep cuts instead of fine ones. His sheer size seemed an insult to the orderly. Maybe Alfred's apologies were his way of shrinking himself.

After we broke up all the dirt clods in the field, Alfred had us plant every kind of food: corn, yellow squash, carrots, leaf lettuce, cabbage, snap peas -- an abundance of vegetables, enough to feed the whole asylum. It did me good to be tired and dirty at the end of the day. I almost felt like my old self. I think it helped Ruth too, although the difference in her was harder to spot. She had an awful sickness she couldn't shake and we couldn't find the plants we needed to cure her of it. Matter of fact, we couldn't find much of anything in the way of remedies there.

The orderly let Ruth and me wander around the edge of the woods for a few minutes at the end of every work day so that we could gather what we needed to make Nurse Chick's tonic. After supper, Nurse Chick would meet me at her office with a tea pot full of bubbling hot water. I'd grind up some leaves and bruise a root or two into it. I knew none of it was going to make a bit of difference, so I worked up a pretty good snake-oil salesman pitch. I reminded her the tonic was part of a treatment process that would take weeks to calm her palsy. I told her we'd change the recipe along the way to make sure it fit what her body needed. She'd have to be patient, I'd say. Patient.

Ruth and I breathed outside air four hours a day for two weeks, and that orderly breathed down our necks every minute. I was sure it wouldn't be long before he'd look down at a chicken wing he was gnawing on for a moment too long. When he looked up, Ruth and I would vanish into the trees, bound for Livingston Hollow.

| RUTH'S PETER LIVES ON |

We were planting one day when Ruth whispered a secret to me from across her row. She said, "Peter's with us."

"I guess it's true what they say," I said. "The dead stay with us long as we keep them in our hearts." I wanted to move on from this topic quickly since I was sure any mention of Peter's name made tiny cracks in Ruth's heart. I knew it did in mine.

Ruth shook her head no at me. "In the flesh."

Now at this point it occurred to me that my dear Ruth might have come out of her tree, so I handled her gently. "Ruth, have you lost your mind? We both saw Peter drop dead in the snow." I grabbed her hand hard like I could squeeze the crazy out of her. "I can't undo it, but I'm working on a way to get you back to the Hollow where you can at least lay flowers on the ground where your husband's buried. Don't go batty on me now, Ruth."

"He's in here," Ruth pointed at her belly. Then she said it plainly. "I got a bun in the oven Busy Bee."

My mouth hung open like an idiot's while my mind tried to make sense of what my ears were hearing. Ruth must have picked up on my confusion, because she laid it out for me.

"I got all the signs. I ain't had my monthly curse since we been here. I'm throwing up like nobody's business. Remember those dandelion leaves I tucked into my pocket yesterday?" Ruth said she'd smuggled the leaves back into her room, put them in a necessary pot and peed on them. A few minutes later the leaves broke out in the telltale red bumps that are a mountain woman's way of knowing if she's knocked up.

"Oh Ruthie!" I picked her up and whirled her around until the orderly shouted at us to cut it out. We crouched down over our work in the dirt, our hands still linked. We squealed and giggled quiet as we could and still get the joy out.

"You two hush up 'fore you get us all three thrown into a stewpot." Alfred's face was stern. He looked sideways at the orderly. "That oaf's not gonna put up with all this carrying on. You wanna get locked up in your rooms the rest of the day?"

Ruth and I unhitched our hands. We fell quiet. I was so full of happiness I overflowed. I knew better than to make a fuss again, so I was quiet about it. I sang in a soft voice, just loud enough for Ruth to hear: "Hush-a-by baby on the tree top, when the wind blows the cradle will rock."

Ruth laughed so hard she fell on her ass in the dirt. Lucky for us the orderly was busy trying not to choke on a whole ham biscuit he'd shoved into his greedy mouth. He didn't notice a thing.

Ruth said we had to keep her baby a secret. She was afraid they might make plans to give him to a rich family in town, like what happened to Jenny McConville's boy.

I agreed. "I don't trust that Nurse Chick," I said.

"I'm so darn tired," Ruth said. "And there ain't a crumb I swallow that don't come back up. It's awful hard for me to work out here."

"We could tell Alfred. I trust him. He'd take it easy on you if he knew."

"No. I can't take no chances Bee. Swear on Peter's grave you won't tell."

"I won't, Ruth. I won't. Don't get so worked up. It's not good for your baby."

"My baby." She said it like it was a beautiful dream she woke up and found out was real. "My baby."

I swore to myself I'd get Ruth out of there before the baby came. Hell, if I was honest about it I knew I had to get her out before Chick was any the wiser. I wouldn't be the cause of any more heartache for Ruth. I was her sworn protector.

"SOMETIMES A MAN CAN'T LIE DOWN NO MORE..."

Geraldine McConville sent word to me through Alfred. Her message was welcome as a Phoenix, risen from the ashes and come to bear me home. You remember she was the nine-year-old, ten by then, I taught while Mama tried to help her mother Jenny learn to read. She and her mama were on the morning work crew (I came out with Ruth afternoons). Alfred knelt down in the row next to the one I was planting and said, "I got a young girl on my other crew, seen you from a distance when you were coming and she was going. Says she knows you from home, but asked me to make sure first. The only problem is I'm supposed to say some words to you 'bout a snake. I can't for the life of me recall what they are. I'd swear it was something 'bout wanting to be friendly with the snake, but who in his right mind would want that? No, that don't make no sense."

The words came to me easily. I couldn't spit them out fast enough, this proof of my own true self Geraldine wanted. "And I wished he would come back, my snake," I said. "For he seemed to me again like a king, like a king in exile, uncrowned in the underworld."

"That's them!" Alfred looked sideways at the orderly who was busy whittling meat from a chicken bone with his eye teeth. "Those are some suspicious words, you ask me," Alfred said. "No good can come from talking 'bout snakes and the devil's house. But that young girl's not got an evil bone in her body, so I know it's just child's foolishness. How you know her?"

Geraldine wasn't in front of me, but I could see her just the same. She was staring too long at the pictures in The Velveteen Rabbit, like maybe she could find a way to cross over its pages and be a new part of the story. The little girl who saved the rabbit from its fiery end. Before I could answer Alfred, I started to cry. Once I let the tears come I couldn't stop them.

"God help me, Nurse Chick gonna string me up," Alfred said, only he called her by her real name, not the nickname I used for her. "Whatever's gotten into you, you'd best get it together 'fore you get us noticed."

Even Ruth, who was feeling particularly sick that day, seemed to rise from her nauseous, pregnant stupor, like a mountaintop out of a wooly fog, long enough to give me a bewildered look.

I kept promising Alfred I was going to stop my bawling, then a new squall would hit. When he spoke to me, his words were gentle. "Okay, alright, don't worry yourself over it," he said. "Why don't you tell me 'bout how you got here. Maybe that'll get you right. Getting fired up always helps me get my feet underneath me again."

So I did. I told him everything while we tucked tiny seeds into beds made from mounded earth. We worked our way down four long rows before I got to the part about Mama's deal with Rowler. Alfred sucked air in through his teeth hard enough to make a whistling sound. When I got to the part where I got Peter killed and his house burned down, I saw Alfred's axe-hewn face go soft as half-churned butter.

"That ain't your fault, girl," he said. "They knew the stakes. I'd bet money it made them feel good to go against those state men, 'stead of rolling over."

"Alfred, I'm the one made this awful mess, then I dropped it on their doorstep," I said. "I got Peter killed trying to save my own hide."

"I'm sorry 'bout Ruth's husband, but he made up his own mind. Look here Miss Bee -- that what Miss Geraldine calls you? You're a young lady so maybe you don't know, but sometimes a man can't lie down no more. It don't matter to him how bitter the fruit is he's 'bout to reap."

That was the first time anybody but Ruth had called me Bee since I left the Hollow. Hearing it brought me back to myself a little. I asked Alfred what he meant about bitter fruit. He thought on it a long time before he spoke. Then he told me this story about the son he had and lost:

"I had a boy," he said. "Eighteen years on this earth. He was special, that boy. Had a fire in him like his mama's got, the kind that drives folks to get things done. Freddie was the only child God blessed us with. We socked away all the money we would've spent putting food in our other young'uns mouths if we'd had 'em, 'so that we saved enough to pay for half of his tuition at Howard -- that's a Negro university up in Washington. He won a scholarship for the rest.

Freddie got an extra helping of brains the day they was passing them out. He was smart as me and his mama put together. But he was proud. Too proud. Sometimes a good lookin' Negro woman can get away with pride, but not a man. 'Specially not one who stood out like Freddie. He wasn't as thick as me on account of his early age, but he cut a fine figure, tall and solid. The white boys in town made it their business to ride Freddie. I guess they thought it was their job to keep him from getting too big for his britches.

It wasn't 'til he turned eighteen and shot up and out like a weed -- I swear he grew a good foot and a half in a year -- that the grown white men noticed him. He had some scrapes with them here and there, but he kept his head down like I taught him, so mostly they let him alone. Then word got around that Freddie was going to college. There's a lot of white men 'round here ain't been to college, so they didn't cotton to a Negro boy going. Must have seemed uppity. They got it in their heads he thought he was better than them. Problem was, they were right. He knew he was better.

Two weeks before he was set to leave for school, he walked his girl into town to buy her a Coca-Cola and some peanuts. Outside the store, a white man took the Coca-Cola and poured it over Freddie's head. This earned him a good set of laughs from his buddies, so he kept on. He dumped the peanuts on the ground and told Freddie to get down there and eat them up like the dog he was.

Now I done told you how smart my boy was. I'm sure he knew he might could get away with picking up those peanuts by hand 'stead of eating them, if he stayed quiet and didn't meet the white man's eyes. He might have been kicked or pushed down, then they would have moved on. But he did something else entirely. He looked that white man square in the eye and said, 'You do it.' The white man must not have believed his ears, because he asked Freddie, 'What did you say to me?' And my proud boy, brimming with extra pride in front of his girl, said, 'If you're so set on seeing those peanuts get eaten, you get down there and do it.'

They drug him through town, chained to a pick-up, then hung what was left of him in a pine grove. The sheriff cut him down and brought him home to me and his mama. Nice man, said he was real sorry, but that was it. Said there were no witnesses. Putting those men in jail wouldn't have brought my boy back anyway.

A man makes his own choices Miss Bee. And sometimes, like with my boy and your friend Peter, he just can't lie down no more."

The orderly gathered me and Ruth up to leave as soon as Alfred finished his story. When I looked back at him, Alfred was still kneeling in the spot where I'd left him, one knee in the dirt, the other up where he could lean a forearm on it. His eyes were cast down. Once I got back to my room, I climbed the pipe and looked for him through my window. It was too dark to make him out.

That night, I saw Freddie in a dream. I knew it was him, even though I'd never laid eyes on him, by the way his skin had ripped away in places and left red meat specked with road dirt and gravel. He told me I ought to do something about my situation before I ended up dead as him. Then he cracked open a Coca-Cola bottle, frosty on the outside with cold, and drank it down in three gulps. He made a sound like the drink had satisfied him, but the corners of his mouth stayed turned down and his face kept its sad look.

When I woke up I was more resolved to leave than I'd been when I closed my eyes the night before. I only hoped I'd have a chance to speak with Geraldine first, even if her words had to come to me through Alfred. Maybe I could figure out a way to collect her and Jenny and us all leave there together.

| JENNY MCCONVILLE GETS CUT OPEN |

I told Alfred I had a dream about Freddie. I left out the part where he had torn-open flesh. Instead, I said he was smiling and drinking a Coca-Cola. I said he seemed peaceful. Alfred asked me was there anybody with him. He said it comforted him to know Freddie had a whole host of family on the other side waiting for him. For his boy to be dead and alone seemed like two injustices. I told Alfred there were too many colored faces around Freddie to count and that they were all laughing and carrying on like they were having the time of their lives (can you say that about dead people?). Alfred exhaled hard on account of he'd held his breath waiting for my answer. Of course, you and I know Freddie was alone and not as much at peace as unsettled, but it didn't seem right to tell Alfred that.

Alfred said Geraldine and her whole family were at the Colony. He said the government had been rounding up the poorest Hollow folk and bringing them to the asylum, for no other crime than not having coins enough to fill a mason jar.

Geraldine and I talked to each other in Alfred's voice. Our conversations stretched over days, since we had to wait for Alfred to relay our messages. I asked Alfred to find out who brought Geraldine's family to the Colony. I had my suspicions, so I described Rowler. Alfred said Geraldine recognized him from the picture I drew with my words. Rowler had been at her house, bossing that lawman with the skunk stripe in his hair. Franklin had been too drunk to put up much of a fight. Jenny just kept asking for assurances that the family would be kept together. Rowler made a persuasive sales pitch. Where he was taking them, he said, they'd have all the food they could eat, a wood stove warm as the tropics and each family member his own bed. It must have sounded to Jenny like a good deal. And it was -- too good to be true.

The first thing they did when the family got to the Colony was separate them. Jenny and Geraldine got to stay together, but Franklin and the boys got put in the men's ward which was in an entirely different building. We shared a dining hall with them, but the men and women ate at different times, so the family wasn't even together at meals. Alfred said Jenny didn't let Geraldine get farther than an arm's length away from her, like she had to be ready to snatch her child up out of harm's way at any time.

Then the day came they took Jenny in for surgery. Alfred said the doctors came by Jenny and Geraldine's room and were talking about cutting on Geraldine. Jenny talked them out of it: said Geraldine was just a child and volunteered herself to go in Geraldine's place. I guess they took her up on her offer. Jenny made Alfred promise to look after Geraldine since she'd be coming out on the work crew alone for a few weeks while Jenny healed. Alfred was real fond of Geraldine. He told Jenny he wouldn't let anything happen to her girl on his watch.

Alfred was Geraldine's keeper and I was Ruth's. That tiny lima bean inside her had walloped Ruth good. She lied and told Chick it was her womanly time so she could stay back in bed for a few days. If she'd been up to it, we might have made a break for it. That peckish orderly had started leaving me alone with Alfred. He walked me out to the field (and finished a sandwich on the way), told Alfred to send me back in time for supper, then turned and high-tailed it back to the indoors. When I delivered the day's herbal concoction to Nurse Chick, I asked her if he'd be back the next day. She said no, she needed him inside to help with a new load of patients that came in.

"I realized how foolish I've been, worrying that you'll run off," she said. "The mountains you're from are close to sixty miles from here." She cocked her head like she might see something different if she looked at me sideways. "I'm not sure you'd leave if you had the chance. I think you want me to help you improve your standing. Don't worry. I'll expunge every bit of hillbilly in you. Do you know what expunge means?"

I let her explain 'expunge' to me -- even though I was well aware of its meaning -- so as not to disturb her picture of me as a bumpkin in need of a good scrubbing up.

"You'll be a better person when you leave here," she said, after she finished her vocabulary lesson.

I'd been thinking hard about how to get Ruth and me back to the

Hollow. Ruth had cousins on the mountain. If I could get her to them, I figured they'd hide her until the law lost interest. I could lay low for a few days, pack up whatever food and clothes I could find in other folks' left-behind houses, then head out to somewhere new. But the ride from the Hollow in the back of the police car took at least an hour. Ruth wasn't in any shape to make that kind of trek on foot. We could have tried to hitch it back, but hanging around the road would have been the fastest way to get rounded up and brought back to where we started from.

In the meantime, Chick was pretty pleased with the arrangement. Her with a lifetime supply of mountain remedies for her palsy and us with no place to go. And even though I was bringing her bootless concoctions that couldn't possibly do her a bit of good, she swore the teas and balms I brewed soothed her palsy. "Wednesday's tea had me feeling better than I have in years," she said. "I want you to make it for me again tomorrow." I didn't tell her Wednesday's tea was mostly made with plain old grass. What had her going was probably the dirt I threw in for good measure. Seemed like the worse the medicine tasted, the more she was convinced it worked.

| TORCH TRIES TO SPRING ME |

Torch came for me every day for thirteen days. He showed up at the same time every afternoon, my guess is after he was finished sorting mail at the store and whatever other chores his Daddy had given him. I was surprised Hiram let him borrow the pickup, or maybe he was sneaking off without his daddy knowing. He left without me quietly most days, but the last day he came was an entirely different story. The orderlies had to all but kill him to get him to move on without me.

Right after I heard the sound of the lock grinding closed that morning (the orderlies locked me in after breakfast, until it was time to go out to the fields), I heard a sound I wasn't accustomed to. It wasn't the muffled shuffle of soft-soled patient shoes, or the metal jangle of an orderly's key chain, or even the shrieks of one of those truly around-the-bend patients who actually belonged in a loony bin. It was my name -- only someone was screaming it so loudly my door just about rattled off its hinges. As soon as I heard it a name was on my lips and I screamed back: "Torch!"

In an instant, Chick's shrill whistle's call brought orderlies pounding down the hall. I tried to reach the transom window over my door to lay eyes on the goings on. I couldn't pull myself up high enough, but I didn't need to. I could tell what was happening from the sound of it. There was the smack of Torch's fists against the orderlies' snapping noses and jaws. I know Torch had the upper hand at first because the whimpers weren't his. Torch finished off the first men, then a few more rolled up. He would have finished them off too if it weren't for the pipe. I couldn't see it, but I knew what it was because it gave off a tell-tale hollow metal ring when it hit him. The orderlies who were still standing dragged Torch down the stairway. He was unconscious or dead, because his boots smacked every step on the way down to the front door. I shimmied up my window pipe in time to see them load him into his daddy's truck and push it out the front gate.

He had worn his only dress shirt -- the white one with the pearlized buttons. He probably thought he could talk me out if he handled himself right. When they put him in the truck I saw the back of his shirt was stained red with blood the pipe had let loose.

The sight of Torch bleeding and limp was more than I could stomach. I tried to break down my locked door. I wanted to strangle the life out of Chick. I wanted to break my window glass and cut all of their throats with it. But I didn't do any of those things. It was too late to help Torch. I owed it to Ruth to harden my heart and hold myself together. If I got myself carted off to jail or killed, where would Ruth be? My only consolation was knowing Torch must have been alive or they would have buried him to hide the body, instead of loading him into his truck.

I sank down onto the floor of the place I could not leave. I sobbed until my head hurt from the heaving of it, then I sang a soft song I hoped might calm my fit. The only one I could think of was the one Peter sang at the corn shucking, one of the last times we were all happy together -- before the government's crimes against us.

Was in the merry month of May
When flowers were a bloomin',
Sweet William on his death-bed lay
For the love of Barbara Allen.
As she was walkin' through the fields,
She heard the death bells tolling,
And every toll they seemed to say,
"Hard-hearted Barbara Allen."
She looked east, she looked west,
She saw his corpse a-comin'.
"Lay down, lay down the corpse," she said,
"And let me gaze upon him."
"O mother, mother make my bed,
O make it long and narrow,
Sweet William died for me today,
I'll die for him tomorrow."

| GERALDINE'S NEAR DEATH |

The day after poor Torch took a beating, I found out they'd killed Geraldine, or near about. Turned out those doctors were lying when they told Jenny they'd take her for surgery and leave Geraldine be. They took Jenny alright. Then, as soon as she was under the ether, they went back and collected Geraldine. It must have been their plan all along.

Alfred broke down when he told me. He said something I wouldn't believe, except Alfred struck me as somebody who wasn't prone to exaggeration. He said the doctors were cutting people open and making it so they couldn't have babies.

"They got a name for it," he said. "Yew-jen-icks or some such thing. Means they don't want you Hollow folks muddying up the country with your lowly young'uns. I reckon they'd do it to colored people too if they didn't need our sons and daughters to do the work white folks think they're too good for."

Why on earth they'd think to cut the womanhood out of a girl too young to use it yet was beyond me. Alfred said the orderlies told him Jenny got back to the room first. She kept asking when Geraldine would be back from lunch. The orderlies didn't answer because they didn't want to deal with the dust-up they knew was coming. Of course, when they carried Geraldine back in on a stretcher all hell broke loose.

Poor Jenny got so worked up, she rolled out of her bed and tried to crawl to her girl. I guess Jenny ripped her stitches because one of the orderlies told Alfred she was bleeding to beat the band. They had to give her a shot of something to calm her down and even then it took two of them to drag her back to the doctor so he could sew her up again.

Jenny came out alright once the doctor put back the stitches she'd torn out, but Geraldine came down with a fever. Alfred said one of the orderlies came and told him he wasn't likely to get his morning work crew back anytime soon. "The mother won't leave the girl," the orderly said, "and it looks like the girl ain't gonna make it. The boys and me got bets going on what's gonna happen to the mother when the girl croaks. 'Bout half think she's gonna will herself dead, the other half -- the half I'm with -- say she'll pull through. Those mountain folks make kids at about the same pace as rabbits, so they don't tend to get too torn up when they lose one. That mama'll snap back. She'd try to push out another pup if the doctors hadn't fixed her."

Alfred is beside himself. "They act like ya'll ain't their own people, cut by God from the same cloth," he said. "Miss Geraldine's just a child. What's she done to deserve this? At my age, I thought nothing could surprise me no more."

I wasn't surprised. If they'd take our homes and shoot our people dead in the snow, what was to stop them from snatching some of our inside parts? Back then, I would have picked giving them a few of my organs over losing the home Daddy built and all my memories of him to those park rangers and their torches. I was afraid after enough time had passed, I wouldn't remember how, after the spring thaw, the waters of Brokenback Run made a tinkling sound like pieces of broken glass tossed around in a sack, or that the whole Hollow smelled like apples in the fall. The only pictures I had of Daddy were in my head. What if they faded a little with every mile I moved away from his homeplace, and a little more every day I wasn't breathing in the same air that passed through him while he was living. Alfred accused me of having a heart cold as January snow, since I hadn't shed the first tear over Geraldine. I guess I didn't have it in me to cry about anything else. All I could think was that if I didn't get me and Ruth out of there fast, we might be the next ones on the doctors' table. That much Alfred agreed with.

"We got to get you away from this place," Alfred said. He'd put together everything I needed to head out the next day. He hid a bag in the shed with some supplies in it. Millie, she was Alfred's missus, packed enough cornbread and ham to last a few days. She packed a blanket in the bag and she put a set of her very own clothes in there for me to change into. She told Alfred I'd better get out of my patient suit quick or I'd be so easy to spot they'd have me back here before I could say freedom. Alfred and Millie thought of almost everything. Alfred planned to tell the orderlies we were working in the south field, that way they wouldn't think anything of it when they couldn't see me from the building. He said by the time they noticed I hadn't come in, I'd be long gone.

I told Alfred there was only one problem. His eyes rolled skyward, like there was a list up there of everything he had to do to get me gone. "We got food, clothes, blankets, a story for the orderlies," he said. "I forget something?"

"I can't go without Ruth," I said.

Alfred's eyes had come down to look at me and now they went skyward again. "Oh Lord," he said. "Miss Ruth too sick to run away from here on foot. It's miles and miles through the woods to anywhere. You got to leave her here, Miss Bee. I don't think she's got it in her to get up and leave."

"I won't go without her Alfred."

"God help me," he said. "Have you even asked her if she wants to go?"

"She'll go," I said. "But you've got to make sure she comes out to the field tomorrow."

"Me?" Alfred threw his hands up. "How in God's name am I gonna do that?"

"I can't get to her at night. She hasn't been coming to dinner and after the chow hall they lock me in my room. You've got to tell Chick you've got a heavy work load tomorrow and you need an extra set of hands."

"Jesus God Almighty. You got a brain, but you don't use it Miss Bee. She'll just send me any old somebody to help." Alfred studied my face. Whatever he saw there convinced him. "I'll have to say Miss Ruth is the only one I can use. I'll think on it and come up with a reason."

"Good. It's settled then," I said.

Alfred grumbled. "We'll need more supplies, and some way to get you and Miss Ruth to where you want to go."

Ruth and I would be Hollow bound in no time. I prayed for us that night. I never put much stock in it, but I'd heard other folks swear by a good visit with God so I figured it couldn't hurt. If I had a lucky rabbit's foot, I would have rubbed that too.

| ESCAPE |

Alfred and his wife Millie put their heads together about a plan to get Ruth and me out. They came up with a whopper.

Millie was going to drive us back to the Hollow in a coal-black death wagon meant for carrying soulless bodies to their earthen beds. Ruth and I were supposed to lay down in coffins in the back like two people who had gone on to the other side. The hearse belonged to Millie's brother. He ran a funeral parlor for colored folks in Luray. Alfred said he had more money than he knew what to do with on account of colored folks take their last offices very seriously. He said the hearse had crimson velvet cushions and a satin ceiling red as blood from a cut hog's neck. All four wheels were gold as anything Midas touched, and the steering wheel was wrapped in calf's skin stained gold. Alfred said the only thing missing was a brass band strapped to the roof playing "Bringing in the Sheaves." He said not to worry about the coffins. When I joked that I was nervous about getting fitted for a wooden overcoat, he said those boxes would be two pillowy cocoons, more agreeable than any bed we'd laid our bodies in at the end of a day.

We were to leave the next day. Alfred said Geraldine had "gone to be with the angels" (his words, not mine). We were quiet for a while after he said it. Then we went on talking about the escape plan he and Millie put together for us. There was nothing more we could do for poor Geraldine.

Ruth didn't come to the field that day. I was fit to be tied since we were supposed to get sprung the next day. Alfred was as mystified as me by her absence. He said Chick had agreed to send her. I was worried about her. I decided I was going to sneak out of the chow hall at breakfast the next day to look for her. I wouldn't rest until I laid hands on my dear, sweet Ruth.

| CHOKING THE LIFE OUT OF CHICK |

I found Ruth in a room on the third floor. I liked to have never found her if I hadn't been able to get it out of an orderly who was willing to trade information for a quick feel. I hope you won't consider your mama a loose woman. Necessity called for it.

When I opened the door to her room, Ruth was lying on a cot with her back to me. She didn't turn when I called her name. "Goddammit Ruth, get your ass out of bed," I whispered loudly from the doorway. "It's time to go." Her side swelled and sank again with the heavy breathing of deep sleep. I crossed the room, irritated. Sick and pregnant or not, I wasn't going to let her miss our chance to escape.

I shook her a little. She let out a loud snort of a snore. I'd had enough of her lazing around. I rolled her over onto her back so I could pull the covers off. A little bit of the Colony's chilled air on her skin ought to help. The waistband of her gray patient suit pants was rolled down to her hips. Underneath, a bloodied bandage stretched over the place where her baby should have been. I put my arms around her and called her name over and over, but she was still under a blanket of ether and I couldn't reach her.

The sight of my Ruth cut open like Jenny and Geraldine sent me into a rage all three Fury sisters together couldn't have matched if they'd come forth from the underworld in the flesh. I went for Chick, consequences be damned. I rushed down the stairs to her office. I called for her by her given name, in a hideous voice that flew on bat's wings. "She is an aberration," I screamed when I reached her hallway and she didn't come to answer me. "She's got palsy. She's diseased."

Chick's wide-eyed face pushed itself through a crack in her office door. She looked like a scared rabbit that had popped up out of its hole and come face-to-face with a hungry fox. "Keep your voice down. Get in here." She pulled me through her half-open door by my sleeve.

"What in God's name do you think you are doing?" She opened the door again long enough to check for eavesdroppers, then shut and locked it.

"You killed him," I said. I don't know if I screamed or sobbed the words. "You cut Ruth's baby out of her and killed him. You bitch. You think I'm going to keep your secret now? Hands that won't do what you want them to. Tremors. Palsy. You're broken. You're sick. If the doctors find out, what will they do? Take away your job? Or will they call you unfit and cut you like they did Ruth and Jenny and Geraldine? You'll say they won't believe me, but they've seen the shakes, haven't they? They just need someone to help them realize what they already know. Maybe they'll decide a lobotomy is what will fix you."

"Shut up, shut up, shut up." She went wild in an instant. She pulled at her hair with her hands, opened her eyes too wide. Then, suddenly as she came undone, she collected herself. She smoothed her hair and closed her eyes for a moment before she spoke. "Keep your voice down. I had nothing to do with Ruth. I don't decide who goes in for surgery. The doctors took her because she kept complaining about her, what did she call it -- her womanly curse. It's that stupid hillbilly's own fault for not telling us she was pregnant."

I had her throat in my hands before I knew I'd gone after her. Her neck was a living thing apart from her -- a snake, flexing and writhing beneath the crush of my fingers. I aimed to kill it. To kill her. A knock came at the door. I let loose of her neck with one hand and put it over her mouth. Lucky for me she had locked us in. The person on the other side turned the knob but the bolt kept him out.

The interruption brought me back to my senses. If I killed Chick, I'd spend the rest of my life here or in jail. I wasn't sure which was worse. Ruth was still alive. I was responsible for her. And Torch. I wanted to see Torch alive and whole so badly it hurt my heart.

I let go of my hold on Chick. She gasped. She stroked her neck. "You're fine," I said. "Which is better than you deserve."

When she opened her mouth to holler for help, only a croak came out. "Go ahead and call them," I said. "The sooner they get here the sooner I can tell them about how you can't control your own body. How you've been sending me and Ruth out to the field to bring back mountain medicine to calm your twitching. Maybe they'll lock you up here in the Colony with the rest of the epileptics and feebleminded."

She leaned back in her chair. "Tell me what you want," she said.

"First tell me what happened to Torch. Did they kill him?"

"Who's Torch? Do you mean that boyfriend of yours who kept showing up like a bad penny? They knocked him out and left him in his car outside the gates. He woke up with a bad headache, that's all. Visitors aren't allowed. I told him as much, but he was obstinate. He was creating a disturbance. I can't allow disorder. No, absolutely not. He had to be removed."

"I'm going to lay the truth about you out for everyone to see. I figure after our little exchange here it'll be pretty hard for you to hide your tremors." I laughed. "Look at you. Your right eyelid is twitching more than a dime-a-dance girl."

Chick pulled a hand mirror out of her desk drawer. "One must always keep up one's personal appearance," she had said once during our lessons. "Let's just calm down, shall we? There's no need to go flying off the handle," she said after she saw her eyelid jump. "I'm sure we can reach some kind of understanding. What can I do to persuade you to practice a lady's discretion?"

"To hell with being a lady," I said. "I'm a Hollow girl and proud of it." Now the right-hand corner of Chick's mouth was in a spasm too. She tried to hold it still with her fingers. I kept talking. "The only way you can guarantee my mouth will stay shut is to let me out of here."

"You know I can't do that. It's not up to me who stays and who goes. You were put here because you attacked that state man. If you were older they would have put you in jail with the rest of the criminals. You won't get out anytime soon."

"Then I guess the doctors will get an earful. The longer I'm here, the more of them I can tell."

"Frankly, I'm at a loss. You, Miss Livingston, are an ungrateful brat. I've kept you off the surgeries list and this is the thanks I get?"

"If you kept me off the list at all, it was only because you didn't want to go without your medicine while I rested up afterward."

Chick slumped into her chair with all the grace of a weary ploughman come day's end. She rested her elbows on her desk and cradled her head in her hands. She was quiet for so long I took to staring at a redbird hopping on her window ledge. When she slammed her fists down on her desk, I was so startled I nearly jumped out of my skin. "You'll escape," she said.

I wondered to myself what sorcery this was, that she could read my mind and know what Alfred and me were planning. Then I realized her words weren't meant as an accusation. She thought this was her idea.

"You can go out to meet that colored man Alfred," she said. "I won't send the orderly to get you until dark. That should give you enough of a head start."

"What about Ruth?"

"Don't be foolish. She'll never make it on foot. She's just had surgery. You'll get caught. You'll be right back here within a day."

"Let me worry about that. Anyway, I won't leave without her."

"Will the Negro raise the alarm when you run off?"

"No," I said.

"He'd be a good one to take the blame for this," she said. She smiled, pleased with her own sharp mind.

"If you try to pin this on him, I'll hear about it. You mark my words I will. I'll be sure to send a letter to Doc Smythe about your health troubles." I'd seen Doc Smythe in the halls, always with a gaggle of other doctors hanging on his coat tails, saying yes sir, no sir. It didn't take a genius to figure out he was the boss. I knew my threat would get Chick's attention.

"Friends with the Negro, are you? Just as well. People from the same low station should look out for each other I suppose." I know she meant to insult me, but I took her words as high compliment. "So be it. There's just one thing you haven't thought of, missy. I've come to rely on those remedies of yours. Maybe it's worth the risk to keep you around to brew them up for me."

"Anybody can make those," I said. It was true. I'd just been throwing whatever was within arm's reach into her teas and balms. They only worked because she believed they did. "I'll write up the recipes, draw pictures of the plants I use. You can get Alfred to mix them up." I figured giving the made-up recipes to Alfred, and filling him in on Chick's ailments, would protect him in case she ever changed her mind about going after him.

Chick passed me a piece of paper and a pencil and told me to get started. Something about it felt wrong, like I'd be giving up a great deal of my upper hand once those recipes were handed off. "You can bet your britches I'm not giving them to you now," I said. "I'll leave them with Alfred. Once we're gone and he's clear of the blame, he'll start brewing up the remedies for you." I looked for holes in my plan and couldn't find any. I felt good about it.

She studied me. "If Alfred doesn't have those recipes, I'll see to it he takes the fall for your escape. He'll get thrown in jail for it. He'll rot in there because of you."

"He'll have the recipes," I promised. "You keep your trembly mitts off Alfred."

So it was done. Ruth's baby was gone. All I could do now was get her out of there. All the years Ruth and Peter asked God for a baby and never got one, they never stopped trying. Isn't that the kind of faith God wants from folks but so rarely ever gets? How could he have let that baby get lost? My heart was broken for Ruth. For myself, too, truth be told. I would have liked to hold a little Peter in my arms and fuss over him. Or a little Ruth. Oh a tiny baby with Ruth's yellow curls! I was so sorry for that child who never was. I was so sorry for my Ruth.

| A LAWMAN STOPS THE ESCAPE |

I told Alfred about my talk with Chick. He whistled at the part about him holding onto the recipes until he was sure Chick wasn't going to put the blame on him and said, "You drive a hard bargain, don't you girl?" Then he smiled bright as day. I was sorry to be leaving him. I told him they'd cut Ruth open, so we'd have to let her rest up for a week before we made our escape. I didn't tell him about the baby. It seemed too awful to mention.

Exactly one week later, Ruth leaned on me for our walk out to the fields. Soon as we got there, Alfred cracked himself in the temple with a heavy metal spade rusted red as clay. I was sure he was going to keel over when he took to his knees right away, but he never did. He squinted at me through blood that striped his face red and said he was going to tell the Colony's ghouls that I knocked him out and made off with Ruth. He said he wouldn't tell tales on me if he thought it would get me into hot water, but he said no one would get too worked up about a white girl hitting a colored man.

I worried about what would happen if someone figured out he'd helped us. Alfred said not to. If he lost his job, he and Millie wouldn't starve. They had people to look after them. At least with the recipes, and knowing about Chick's sickness, he had a backstop. Alfred told me not to dwell on it. "I ain't doing this just for you," he said. I must have looked puzzled, because he grunted like he had better things to do but explained anyway: "All those years I thought I was teaching my boy how to live in this world," he said. "It was him who schooled me. I know now a man's got to stand up once in a while, or he loses what makes him a man. I'm proud to say this was my plan so if need be, I guess I'll take what trouble comes with it."

I wish I could have thought of something to say to Alfred as good as what's written in books. Some version of Dickens came to mind. "It is a far, far better thing that you do, Alfred, than ..." But those words would have made it sound like I believed myself to be as inspiring as Lucie, and I was under no such illusions. Not to mention the fact that I hoped Alfred's sacrifice wouldn't compare to the direness of Sidney Carlton's. In the end, I could only say, "I'm right grateful for what you've done for us, Alfred," like some stupid country girl who didn't know the proper way to talk. Alfred smiled and said not to thank him yet, since a lot could still go wrong. I told him to be listening, cause I'd send him another thank you on the wind as soon as we set foot in the Hollow. He said that would be just fine.

Millie was waiting for us on the main road outside the asylum grounds right where Alfred said she'd be. Ruth and I had to pick our way through a patch of poison ivy to get to her, but I figured some itchy prickles were better than strutting down the asylum's driveway like two cocky roosters and getting ourselves hauled right back to the coop we came from.

I only saw her for two short moments: first when we climbed into the coffins, then when we got out -- but I can tell you Millie looked like the Freddie in my dream, or rather he was the spitting image of her, with a face half taken up by eyes outsized and despairing, that smoked with centers made up of secret embers.

Millie's toughness made Alfred look like the soft one of the pair. There was some godawful fierce hate in her look. I knew it wasn't aimed at us and it was my strong desire to keep it that way. Every order she barked at us we followed. "Take your shoes off 'fore you get in the coffins," she said. "The next dead folks who use 'em don't want 'em stained with Colony mud. It's unlucky." I helped Ruth into her fancy casket and Millie tucked me into mine. Those boxes were waxed shiny and felt silky as a baby rabbit's pelt inside. She told us to hold still and not let any part of ourselves leak outside of our death boxes the whole ride.

"You'll be tempted to open 'em to let the air in," she said. "Don't. There's air enough in there to last you for this ride. If the Colony gets word you're out, they might get ahold of the police in time to set up road blocks in case you try to hitch your way home. The police see a cracked open coffin they gonna get real curious." She pinched her lips with her fingers like she was trying to recall a lost thought. She was quiet for a long minute, then it came to her. "No talking in the coffins. You get to chatting, you're liable to bring out whatever spirits still hanging around in this hearse looking for company. And I don't cotton to hearing noises coming from back here where the dead lay. Makes my skin creep." Handing out all those directions must have calmed her nerves, because she went from fidgety to still and closed us up in our coffins with all the sureness of a mama tucking in two children.

It only took a few minutes riding in that tight, unlit coffin to make me hungry for light and air. Alfred was right. It was soft and puffy as a cloud in there. It would have been restful, but I couldn't move my arms more than a few inches and the coffin's cushioned top swelled in my face like it wanted to smother me. The air inside seemed bad. I couldn't fill my lungs, so I started to suck at the air in short bursts which only made matters worse. Millie was way up front, focused on the road. I took a chance she wouldn't see, and let my fingers crawl through the crack between the lid and the coffin to prop it open. It was getting late. Waves of night were lapping at the dropping sun, but enough light seeped into my resting place to let me know I was still alive to see it. Millie's half-down window up front let in the chilled outside air. It eddied around me like a river's whirlpool. Right away my breath fixed itself and got long and even again.

Soon enough I was sorry I'd disobeyed Millie. I saw the red lights after we'd been driving for a half hour. A car pulled up close enough behind us that its headlights lit up Ruth's coffin and mine. I pulled my coffin shut too quickly and smashed my fingers between the lid and the box. That's when the red lights started their angry whizzing and the patrol car screamed its siren at us. Millie drew the hearse to a quick stop. I needed to lift the lid to free my fingers, but I could hear a man's voice coming from outside Millie's window and I didn't dare move. The voice was puffed up in the way that, in my experience, meant its owner wanted to show somebody how important he was.

He sounded much younger than Millie, but he called her girl. "What are you doing cruising around in a hearse this late, girl? You niggers burying your dead in the dark now?"

"No sir, officer," Millie said in a weedy voice, not at all like the powerful one she'd used with us. "I got some fresh ones in the back, just passed over. I'm taking 'em to my brother's funeral home to get prettied up for their viewings tomorrow."

"Well you got one trying to escape."

"Escape, sir?"

"You heard me girl," the officer said. "There's fingers sticking out of one of those coffins you're toting." A flashlight's beam circled our coffins once, then left us alone.

Millie didn't miss a beat. "I thought as much," she said. "I got one's been setting since yesterday. Sweet old woman lived alone with no kin left 'cept a no-good daughter off whoring around Richmond. Neighbors went to look after her soon as they realized they hadn't seen her outside in a few days. Found her upright in her chair, dead as a doornail. The stiffness had already set in. We had to break her legs at the knees to get her in the box. Wasn't easy. She's a big woman -- all swol' up from eating too much fried okra and sweet potato pie. I reckon we're gonna have to break her arm or her fingers one. Won't take but a minute. You got a billy club you could use? You just smack until you hear something snap. Course, you'll want to cover your nose and mouth with a hanky so the smell doesn't get to you."

"Jesus," the officer said. "I don't want nothing to do with no dead, bloated nigger. You move along now. You can fix what needs fixin' when you get to your nigger funeral home."

Millie waited for the patrol car lights to pass us before she pulled back onto the road. I thought she might cuss us from her seat up front, but all I heard was her thanking God and Jesus for watching over us. I'm sure Millie has a special fellowship with the man upstairs, but if you ask me it was her fast talking got us out of trouble, not some magic wand waved from heaven.

A day later, and Ruth and I were two mice, sprung from our traps by humble lions. Alfred would barely accept my thanks back at the Colony and Millie was no different. When she dropped us on a back road on Ragged Mountain, she shooed us into the woods before I could get out more than a few words about how grateful we were. "Go on, now," she said. "'Fore somebody comes along and gets to wondering 'bout how you two dead folks came back to life in this here hearse."

We woke up to Hollow light in the morning, bright and unclouded. Everything down on level land, at the Colony at least, was blurred. Up mountain it was clear -- even in a haze there was the glow of a green field, the red flash of an apple. I was breathing easier, even though I knew we were hunted. Ruth was her old self. She had shaken the devil that had a hold of her. She snuck into the Weston's barn (they were long gone, to where I didn't know) and brought back an old blanket and some rope. She said we could use the rope to make rabbit snares and have us a coney stew. The rope was too thick and I didn't dare start a fire to make stew and announce our presence to the world, but I didn't say any of that to Ruth. I was so glad to have her back I didn't want to spoil it. The blanket would keep us warm on cool spring nights, so that was something.

I went skulking around the woods, looking for any sign of Ruth's people. She had two cousins over in Corbin Hollow I could have turned her over to, but I watched their houses for hours and didn't see hide nor hair of any living thing. Could everyone be gone? It seemed strange that entire communities could sink away like Atlantis into the sea.

I had to think on a plan. I could leave -- head out on foot as far as the train yard, then hop my way to anywhere. Ruth couldn't keep up, so I had to find a place for her first. I half wished Alfred and Millie were around to tell me what to do. My brain couldn't seem to come up with the answers to my questions. The only thing I could think to do was work my way down to MacArthur's Store, find some way to get Torch's attention and send word to Ruth's people through him. Seemed like word of everything that happened around the Hollow reached his ears sooner or later, so he was sure to know where they were.

The trick would be not getting myself caught. I knew the park rangers were busy wiping away any remembrance of the people who'd lived in the hollows. I had to be careful to stay clear of them. They were sure to be hanging around MacArthur's and I sure as hell didn't want to end up back in Nurse Chick's claws or Rowler's.

| RUTH IS LOST |

I failed Ruth. I came close to sewing up a tolerable ending to our story together, hers and mine. The solution I'd come up with was a tarnished brass ring at best, but I wanted to reach it no less than if it had been the holy grail itself. I fell far short.

I went down to MacArthur's Store in the hours between night and morning, when darkness still provides cover, when night watchmen have drunk themselves into a sleepy stupor and the morning scouts are still in bed enjoying their women. I couldn't leave a note in my own hand for Torch, in case someone else got to it first, so I stopped at the McConville's place on my way. I cut a few of Jenny's pride and joy rhododendron flowers from the bush in front of the house and snatched a piece of one of Franklin's smashed-up, left-behind whiskey jugs. On the store's porch, I left the flowers to wilt under the clay triangle that still stunk of white mule. Then I hurried back to the McConville's and waited to see if Torch could decipher my clues.

When I got back, I looked around for some forgotten whiskey. I figured a swig or two wouldn't hurt. I had no luck until I remembered Franklin kept an emergency bottle buried behind the necessary house where nobody would dare go digging around. There it was, a hundred paces from the shitter just like he'd whispered to me once after he'd knocked back too much of the stuff. I drank the bottle half empty, then made my way back to the house and crawled into the upstairs bed Geraldine had shared with her brothers. I wanted to lay down with a smell I remembered from before. The corn husks were sharp in my back and the blankets were too thin to offer much padding, but I was so bushed a hundred elephant tusks in my ribs wouldn't have kept me awake. It hadn't nearly been long enough when Torch woke me with his hollering.

"What on God's green earth you doing asleep, Bee Livingston?" His voice was too loud. "You're laying around up here like some fool who wants to get caught."

"Ease up, Torch," I said before I opened my eyes. "I just needed a little rest."

"How much did you drink? I smelled it on you coming up the ladder."

I opened my eyes and sat up to yell back at him, but instead I started to cry like a stupid girl. I was over the moon to see him alive and in one piece, true, but that was no excuse. I bawled at the Colony in front of Alfred. Now this. I prided myself on holding onto my tears as good as any man, so I was as surprised by my silly outburst as Torch. It must have been the whiskey. Whatever it was, Torch stopped his yelling and sat down next to me in the husks. He stroked my hair and told me not to cry in the same soft voice he'd used when he made me a gift of that honey jar so many months before. When that didn't stop my blubbering, Torch laid his body down next to mine and pulled me in close. He smelled good, and he had a powerful hold that eased my worries.

I must have dozed again. When I came to I saw that Torch had ahold of my left hand. He was studying my fingers like he was trying to memorize the lines around every knuckle. I squeezed his hand.

"I'm sorry," I said. "I don't know what's gotten into me."

"'S okay," he said. "I shouldn't have hollered at you. The sight of you dozing like a kid got me riled up like it was my job to keep you safe." He paused for a minute before he said, "I'm glad to see you. I didn't know when I'd lay eyes on you again."

Torch was full of questions about how I escaped from the Colony. He said he made off with his daddy's truck one night, pretty soon after they took me and Ruth, and hauled ass all the way down there, bound and determined to spring me. The gates were locked, so he hid the truck on a side road and climbed the fence. He watched for me from the woods all the next day with no luck. I told him that was back when Nurse Chick had me locked up like a canary in a putrid coal mine. He said he came back again, bound and determined to get me out but went home a failure. I told him I'd heard it all happen and he was no failure. The orderlies he roughed up licked their wounds for a good week after he got ahold of them.

He said he thought I might die in that place, at their hands or my own.

"I'm still here," I said. "The ones who deserves to be isn't."

"Ruth? Did something happen to Ruth?"

I told him about Ruth and the baby. The more I told him, the more his temperature rose until he finally got so hot he slammed his fist clear through a flimsy spot in the cabin wall. I could see the McConvilles' spring house in the middle of the hole he left, like it was a framed picture.

I broke the news about Geraldine next. Then it was his turn to cry. He looked more man than boy to me now. It rattled me to watch his body buffeted by sobs. He wiped his wet eyes hard with the backs of his hands, embarrassed by what I'm sure he thought was weakness shown.

I kept right on talking. I'd known Torch long enough to know, when he got embarrassed, it was best to move past it fast. "I need your help with Ruth," I said. "She's here with me and I've got to find somebody to look after her."

"I should've known you'd bring her along," he said. "You know they must have been working on a way to get her out of that place soon as the doctors realized the mistake they made. You could've left her behind and they would've sent her back here soon as she healed."

"I couldn't leave her Torch."

"Your goddamned mule's stubbornness is gonna get you in a heap of trouble."

"It already has. I figure I might as well stick with it now and see where it takes me."

"So you want my help with Ruth, is that it?"

"Yeah. Her people from Corbin Hollow have moved on. Do you know where to?"

"One of her cousins sold to the government, managed to get a pretty good deal." Torch raised his eyebrows, impressed by the cousin's accomplishment. "He bought a handful of acres northeast of Sperryville way. Want me to get word to him?"

"I don't want to give him a chance to say no," I said. "Let's just deliver Ruth to his doorstep." I asked Torch if he could steal his daddy's truck again, then I did something I shouldn't have. I lowered my head a little and looked up at him through my eyelashes. I couldn't let him say no. I put my hand on his knee then leaned toward him a little and let my fingers slide up his thigh. Then I said, "please" in as breathy a voice as I could manage.

Torch was no dummy. He saw my game for what it was. It still worked. "Jesus Bee, you're pulling out all the stops. I ought to say no and see what else you'll do." He chuckled. My face must have stayed serious, because when he looked at me again he got serious too. He said, "My old man hid the keys after I came home beaten to a pulp last time. I'll have to find 'em first but, yeah, I'll do it."

I told Torch we'd be ready that night, but he said his daddy had driven the truck to Richmond to visit with a lawyer and wouldn't be back until the next day. We settled on a time to meet the next night, halfway up the road to Mountaintop. Then we split up. He went back to the store and I headed back to our hiding spot behind the Weston's place to tell Ruth the good news.

I met Ruth sooner than I expected, on the path above Thompson's Gorge. I fussed at her for being up walking when she should have been giving her stitches a chance to take. She said it was only a short walk and it would do her mind good. We locked arms.

"Bumble Bee, it ain't your fault what done happened to Peter," Ruth said. "Or the baby." I cried again. Ruth stayed peaceful, serene in her sadness.

I said how sorry I was, told her she'd have been better off without me. She shushed me and said, "You brung me joy so many times when I didn't have none. Ain't no telling what would'a happened if'n you hadn't been there. Peter'd already done told me the only way he was leaving this place was in a pine box. He could'a done a right good job getting himself killed all on his own, and maybe me to boot."

Ruth stopped. I pointed out a rock where she could rest and look out over the gorge. She kept standing. "Bee," she said, "You go off with Torch, you hear?"

"Sure," I said. "Miles will be on his way back to Washington soon. Maybe we could meet up with him. We could get jobs in the city."

"Don't you wait for that city photographer," she said. I could feel a gloom come over me at the thought of forsaking my dreams of traveling the country with Miles. She sensed my bad feelings and said quickly, "I'm sure he's a fine fellow. But Torch's been downright lovesick over you.

You've fallen for him too. Deny it and you'll burn for lyin'."

"Your brain's gone foggy."

"It's the God's honest truth. There's more to love than fairy-tale letters from far off places, Busy Bee. You ain't a girl no more. You got to face facts. That photographer friend of yours ain't here. Torch claimed you even when it meant a whooping. I need to know you got somebody around man enough to look after you."

"Ruth, what are you going on about?"

Ruth backed away from me until she'd reached the rim of a rock that, at its end, ceded to the sky. Shock gummed up my body's works. I could only move slowly, a fly in my own saucer of molasses. I stepped towards her, but her upheld hand was enough to stop me.

"Ruth," was all I could say.

"Bee." Neither of us moved. Our eyes held each other for a while, then she turned and dove into the sky. No sound came from her except the wind's sharp whipping past the dress Millie had loaned her.

My Ruth was gone. I called her mine since there was no one else left to claim her. She had been mine since the day Rowler shot Peter, a sweet albatross hung from my neck as a reminder of my crimes -- heavy, but beloved in a way the mariner's bird was not.

At our camp, there was a note from Ruth. I sat down with it while there was still enough day left to read it by. She used a piece of the paper left over from the stash I stole from the Colony. Her hand must have been sure. Her letters were dark, solid. "My sweet Bee," it said. "This world done finished with me. Peter calls me home."

I wished for more. I wished for a letter so long it would take years to finish -- a book that would deliver new words from Ruth every day until I was ready to close its cover. Instead Ruth was dead and I had no more left of her than I had of Daddy or Peter or Geraldine. So I promised myself I'd write my own book. I told myself I'd put all my people in it and everything I knew about the Hollow the way it was before the government stole every stream and apple tree. I'd put Mama in it. Rowler too, even though I didn't want words about that business with him rubbing up against stories about Torch and me fishing or Geraldine learning to read.

I guess this is that book I promised myself, but it turns out it's not for me. It's for you sweet Amelia. And before it's done you'll read all about how you came to be and why I thought picking the wrong man was the right decision.

| TORCH AND HIRAM ARE NEXT ON ROWLER'S LIST |

I forced myself to climb down to Ruth the next morning as my penance. I found her with her eyes skyward. She watched for Peter to come down and fetch her. I believe he did. I wrapped her broken pieces in the blanket she'd given me days before.

I don't compare myself to divine Prometheus, but I think that morning I knew the pain he felt each time the eagle visited.

I carried Ruth up the steep path to the home she had shared with Peter. I dug the hole in the ground that would hold her. I covered her before Torch showed. He didn't deserve to see her that way.

Torch came carrying a stuffed rabbit made with pieced together velveteen and a lilac bow around its neck -- right off the pages of Geraldine's favorite book. Torch said it was from a catalog his daddy had at the store. He was planning to give it to Geraldine for her birthday.

"I don't know what to do with it," he said.

"We'll bury it," I said. "Next to Ruth." I won't recount Torch's grief over Ruth's death. It wouldn't be right for me to share what belonged to him.

We dug a bunny-sized hole next to Ruth and laid all we had left of Geraldine down in it. Her real body was buried up at the Colony. I hated to think of her there for eternity. She should have crossed over from the Hollow. She should have been a grizzled old biddy -- grandma to a bunch of snot-nosed kids whose names she couldn't remember -- who keeled over in her favorite porch rocker.

I took comfort in knowing Ruth and Peter were with her. They could look after her until her mama came. I wouldn't have gone as far as to say they were all up in some enchanted heaven holding hands and dancing around a May pole or some other silliness. I didn't know what it looked like, but I did get the feeling they were someplace together. I hoped Daddy was there too. He'd be a good father to Ruth and Geraldine and they could stand in for the daughter he left behind.

After we'd laid our loved ones to rest, Torch told me the government wanted Hiram to sell the store. "He wants to negotiate with them government folks for a higher price," Torch said. "Pretty soon they're gonna get tired of his nonsense and just close us down."

"There's no surprise in that," I said. "You knew they weren't gonna kick everybody else out and let you all stay."

"Yeah, I knew it." He brushed his hands over his hair the way I'd seen Alfred do it, the way some grown men do when they're thinking on something, then he said, "Bee, I don't wanna leave my mama behind, all alone in the dirt with city folks stepping over top of her."

"Shit," was all I could think to say. I put my arm around him and leaned my head on his shoulder. He rested his cheek on my uncombed hair. He reached around my waist with one of his burned up hands. "I don't want to leave Daddy either," I said. "We don't have to go yet. Nobody knows I'm here and you and your daddy still have the store. We won't leave until we're good and ready."

"Yeah," he said. Then he repeated my words, "good and ready," like they were our very own proverb.

Miles had been writing since before I got sent to The Colony that I should go down the mountain, try my luck in the city. He said pretty as I was I'd have people falling all over me wanting to give me a chance. Truth be told, I'd dreamed of leaving the Hollow for a long time. When it came down to it though, it wasn't so easy to ditch the place where I'd made every memory I had, good and bad alike. Anyway, I suspected the other city folks might not be as patient as Miles with my bad manners and loose morals.

| HOLLOW FOLKS SEND LETTERS
TO THE GOVERNMENT |

I laid low in the snakes' hibernating hole since it was near about summer and they weren't using it. The rocks up there made good hiding places. Only problem was the snakes thought so too, so I had to watch my step. In general our arrangement worked pretty well. When the sun was up, the snakes spread their scales over the rocks to bathe in its warmth. I spent daylight hours hiding like Bonnie Parker on the run from the law. I stretched my legs in the dark when the snakes were after their supper. If Torch had it his way, I wouldn't move a muscle unless I checked with him first. He came by every night to check on me. I gave him a hard time about hovering like a mama bird, but I liked it.

I hadn't heard any park rangers stomping around my cave yet (they wore boots that trumpeted news of their coming far ahead of when they were within sight). But I knew my days up there were numbered. If the snakes didn't get me Rowler would. Given a choice, I'd have picked the snakes. If I was lucky, it would be neither.

Torch and I planned to head out to the train yard as soon as I had enough money. Torch had taken up a collection of sorts for us. He pocketed some loose change from his daddy's cash box every day, then brought it to me in a tied-up kerchief. Hiram would usually find him out the first day, but Torch said his daddy was so worked up over the government trying to take away his store that he wouldn't notice an elephant sitting on his lap.

He came one night with two pennies and a nickel for my kerchief, ten slices of cured ham and some crackers for supper. After we ate, he told me about the letters. He said folks from across four hollows had written hundreds of them. Every day, a handful of men, women too, came by the store to mail letters to the park authority and our president, Mr. Roosevelt.

The ones who didn't know how to write dictated to Torch and he put their words to paper.

Sal Ales, who sold his thirty acres to the government for two hundred dollars, asked if he could take his roof shingles with him since they were brand new and he'd put a lot of time into making them. Eve Ostriker asked if she and her husband Abe could stay on until Abe passed, since he was in his dotage and not likely to be drawing breath at the same time the next year. Daniel Keane wanted to know when he could take his wife and four young 'uns home to Livingston Hollow. He asked Torch to write that he was thankful for the resettlement house, but there wasn't enough land to farm and he didn't know how he was going to feed his family. Ed Sparr asked for permission to harvest his apple crop in the fall. He asked Torch to write that he knew the government owned his land, but he'd heard they were planning to let the apples rot where they fell. It would be a shame to see a good apple crop go to waste and he could use the money besides. Torch said the government only gave Ed a few hundred dollars for forty acres with a house and a barn and a mature orchard that everybody knew bore some of the best-tasting apples you could sink your teeth into.

Torch said return letters came from Washington, from a man named Tugwell who didn't know how to say anything but no. Torch said what stuck in his craw was how Hollow folks had to ask permission to take what belonged to them. They said please and thank you, polite as can be, to a bunch of criminals who called themselves the government. He said every bit of land had been stolen -- even what was paid for, because nobody got a fair price. And when the park service wrote back and told them no, they couldn't have what was theirs, there was nothing they could do but hang their heads and take it.

| A RUN-IN WITH ROWLER'S MAN WHITMAN |

The calendar may have read June, but it was warm as the hottest August day in the Hollow. On days hot as those, Torch and I used to go lay in Brokenback Run to cool off. I knew he would frown on me going alone when it was light outside, being hunted like I was, but that cold water called me to it. I bargained with myself to justify the risk. I would only stay a few minutes, long enough to get my hair wet and chill the rest of me. I'd be extra careful to stop every few minutes on the walk down and listen for the sound of people. I'd go to an overgrown part of the creek where I could hide quick as a bunny if someone got too close.

I set out in the heat of the day. Torch had told me Rowler, his men and the park rangers had all been hanging around the store afternoons when sister sun was at her worst. He said they'd kick back half a dozen orange Nehis and not pay a dime. Rowler liked to hold the door to the freezer chest open and hunch over it, stealing all the cold air. When Torch caught him with both arms sunk up to the elbows in the icy freezer water, he told Rowler if he didn't close the freezer he'd find himself shut in it. Torch was twenty by then, almost big as Rowler and all muscle besides. Rowler gave him a nasty look, but in the end he did as he was told.

It took me a half hour to cover the ten minute walk to the creek since I tiptoed all the way and stayed off the trail out of sight. The last few minutes were the hardest. I could hear the creek gurgle. The thought of that cool water made me feel hot in my skin. I wanted to take off running and land in the creek with a splash, but I didn't dare.

When I finally made it to the creek bank I slipped in quietly, clothes and all. I figured my wet clothes would help cool me even after I left the water and besides, I didn't want to run through the woods in the altogether if I had to make a quick escape. The stream gave me a jolt when I first lowered myself in on account of it being so cold and me being cooked by the afternoon sun up in the snakes' rocky world. Then a good feeling overtook me like I hadn't had in a long while. Unlucky fugitive that I was, a cold moment in a clear mountain stream was all it took to float hope to the surface.

The water sang to me. The trees joined in when the rare breeze ruffled their leaves. My quiet days in the asylum, locked away from the natural world, helped me appreciate the music of the mountain. It was good to hear it.

Then there was another sound, one I knew might mean danger. Twigs snapping. Dead leaves crumbling. Something was after me or the water, one. I hustled fast as I could under some tree roots and briars that hung over the bank. I waited, thankful the sound of the water running over the creek's rocks covered the sound of my panicked breath. The something that was coming took a few more timid steps toward me and the creek. This was not Rowler, to be sure. I started to relax a little. Then, like a shot, the thing crashed over the bank down into the water not more than a foot away from me. When I saw it was a doe with her fawn, I had a quiet chuckle. After she took a few sips, my eyes met the mother's from under the roots and she froze for a moment before she and her baby bounded away again.

After the false alarm with the deer, I relaxed a little too much. My eyelids grew heavy and I let myself close them -- only for a few minutes, I warned myself. I must have slept for hours, because when I woke up the sun's hard afternoon rays had softened into early evening light. Just as I knew from Torch that the men looking for me took sheltered in the heat, I also knew they came out for a last look every evening.

I scrambled up the bank and off toward the snakes' cave. I switched between walking and running. I was making too much noise and I knew it, but I was anxious to crawl back into the safety of my hiding spot. I almost made it, too. I was a hundred yards away when I came face to face with Rowler's lawman -- the one with the skunk's white shock of hair who was holding me when Rowler shot Peter. I froze just as that mama deer had done when she saw me. I waited for the lawman to shout to let Rowler and the rest of the search party know he'd found me. Then I heard that devil Rowler's voice call in that familiar growl, "Whitman, you see anything over your way?"

"Nothing over here," the lawman I now knew was Whitman hollered back to Rowler. "I'll meet you west of the creek."

"Yeah, okay," came Rowler's answer.

The man called Whitman pulled a parcel from his pants pocket, something wrapped in wax paper, and set it down on the ground slowly, so as not to scare me away. He backed a few steps in the direction of Rowler's voice, then turned and hustled away in a hurry. I grabbed the parcel and ran for the cave. Once I was safe in the darkness of the carved-out rock, I peeled back the wax paper to find an untouched meatloaf sandwich and a ten dollar bill. I was so hungry it was the best sandwich I'd ever put in my mouth. If I had to guess, I'd say Whitman had a nice wife at home who made it. I wonder if she knew it would end up in my stomach. I wonder if he told her about Peter and Ruth and me.

That ten dollars would go a long way. It was three times what Torch and I had tucked away in our kerchief. Torch told me there was a westbound train that ran by the foot of the mountain every month. We'd just missed the last one, but another would come along in less than three weeks. Our plan was to lay some branches across the tracks so the engineer had to stop and clear them. That would give us enough time to climb into one of the boxcars unnoticed, Torch said. Soon, we'd be off.

| ROWLER GRABS TORCH |

After my run-in with the lawman, I promised Torch I wouldn't leave my borrowed cave until after dark, but I got antsy again after two weeks had passed. It was dullsville up there. I had no company, no work to keep me busy -- just a whole lot of sitting to do. I whittled to pass the time (an entire navy of mini canoes and a few snakes because they were the easiest, a pig from a fat chunk of soft pine, and one big wooden pecker that curved a little to the left on account of the branch being crooked). If there'd been a piece of wood big enough, I could have carved Noah's Ark.

A girl can only take so much of that kind of tedium. So I came up with a plan to change my scenery for a day. I snuck down mountain before dawn and hid myself in a deadfall where I could see the goings on at MacArthur's. I'd been feeling down in the mouth for a while. I figured seeing a few folks I recognized might lift my spirits. Maybe if I got lucky a few old coots would take to their pipes on the front porch. I was close enough to be able to make out most of what they said. If I couldn't chew the fat with them at least I could listen.

You may remember me telling you that Torch and his daddy lived in the rooms above the store. From my new den, I saw Hiram's window light snap to before dawn. That man could be about as ornery as Mama, so I got a little edgy at the thought of him tromping around up there. I suspected Hiram hadn't allowed himself to forget his Mrs. for one moment since she'd died. That would make anybody a miserable son of a bitch. Hell, if you'd set foot in the rooms they shared over the store, you'd have thought the woman was still alive. Torch snuck me in there once when his daddy was minding the store, since Hiram didn't care for house guests. In the sitting room, there was a small wooden love seat topped with a baby blue cushion. It was a dainty thing, the kind a woman would pick out. Next to it a pretty, carved side table held up a colorized picture of Torch's mama. Her lips and cheeks were painted a rosy pink. Her dress was stained pink too, even though Torch said it had been yellow in real life. He remembered it well because she wore it every Easter and got buried in it to boot.

I got it in my head that I wanted to sit on the girly love seat, but soon as I bent my knees and started to sink, Torch hollered at me to stop. He said his mama sat on it the day she died. His daddy hadn't let anybody else's behind graze it since. When I looked down at the seat, I swear I could see the heart-shaped indentation of a woman's backside in the cushion. A picture came to me of Hiram on his knees by the chair, crying into his dead wife's ass print. It was a silly picture, but it made me understand him better. I remember seeing Hiram dote on his wife before the fire got her. He used to lift heavy boxes so she didn't have to. There was enough heavy work around the Hollow that women couldn't always be spared it, but she was.

He kept one of the shelves stocked with boxes of a fancy, lavender flower soap she liked. There was still a wardrobe in his bedroom filled with her clothes. And Hiram made Torch sit with him in front of the radio Monday nights to listen to the Rudy Vallee Show like she used to do, even though neither Torch or Hiram ever enjoyed it.

Come daybreak, I was dozing in my hideout. The sound of tires on the store's gravel road woke me. I thought maybe it was out-of-towners stopping for gas until Rowler's Ford pulled in behind them. I could have picked out that car blindfolded, just from the sound of it. The engine had a way of growling like its owner. I figured they were going to grill Torch about my whereabouts, but it turned out I was silly to think Rowler's visit was about me. He and his men had other plans entirely.

Rowler whomped on the store's still-locked door until Hiram came out in his shirtsleeves, unshaven, his hair tousled from sleep. I'd never seen Hiram walk outside without a hat, much less with his face roughened by a night's beard growth and his hair uncombed. When Hiram asked Rowler what the hell all the fuss was about, his voice had an edge to it. But when he saw the four men who had come with Rowler climb out of their cars and stand facing him, he softened his tone. Some of the men in the line stood with their arms by their sides, some with arms crossed, but all of them with blackjacks in hand, the kind policemen use to crack skulls. Rowler told Hiram his time was up. "We're closing this place down today," he said. "You can clear out on your own steam, or we can clear you out."

I was sure that Hiram's brain was busy working out how quickly he could get to his shotgun. I heard him call Torch and I expected he was about to gamble that he and his son could take on five men and win. "The government won't give me a fair price for my store, so I'm not selling," he said. "You tell your bosses I'll turn the place over when they add a few zeroes to that offer of theirs."

"The time for offers is through," Rowler said. "I got the nod to get you out by any means necessary." His lips curled into the same smile I'd seen the day he bartered with my own Mama for sex with me.

Hiram puffed up, ready for a fight. Torch stood behind him. He put his hand on his Hiram's shoulder and whispered something in his daddy's ear that let the air right out of Hiram. Torch looked Rowler in the eye and said, "You got to give us an hour to get cleared out."

"You've got fifteen minutes," Rowler said.

I watched Torch and his daddy load their truck with their belongings. They came out with the love seat first. When it wobbled in their grip, I wanted to run out and help them bear it, but I didn't dare. In the end, they put it down with the outline of Mrs. MacArthur's ass still intact. After a few things from upstairs, they started bringing out boxes from the store.

Rowler stepped in front of Hiram, grabbed a hold of a box of dry goods he was carrying and said, "Time's up."

"Be reasonable, goddammit," Hiram said. "I got hundreds of dollars worth of stock in there."

"You should have thought of that before now, you stupid hick. The State of Virginia has already given this land and what's on it to the federal government, so every last sack of flour belongs to Uncle Sam now."

Hiram let go of the box, balled his fists up and set his jaw. Part of me wanted to see him send a couple of Rowler's little white teeth flying like hail in a storm, but in the end Torch put his arm around his Daddy and walked him to their truck, which anybody with good sense could tell you was for the best. Rowler followed them and handed Torch a slip of paper with what turned out to be an address: 55 Resettlement Road.

"The government set aside a house for you two down with the other hillbillies," Rowler said. "You ought to thank your lucky stars. If it were up to me, I'd throw you in jail."

Torch turned the key, then said over the sound of the engine, "Well then, I guess it's lucky for us the higher ups see you for the jackass you are and don't let you run things. You're planning to sack the store, take what you want? You oughta thank your bosses for throwing you their scraps."

Rowler reached into the truck's open window and grabbed Torch by his shirt. Thank God almighty he lost his grip when Torch hit the accelerator and the truck pulled away.

I had to look down at my hands for a few moments to collect myself. I'd never seen a man big as Hiram look so small. But I think what got me most was seeing Torch put a gentle hand on his daddy's shoulder there in the doorway. That after all the locking horns they'd done over the years there could still be so much love was really something.

When I looked up again, Rowler and his men were traipsing in and out of MacArthur's like it was their very own. Two of them squatted on the front porch steps with a bottle of the whiskey Hiram kept hidden under the counter. They took turns swigging the booze and tearing off pieces of a ten pound ham they'd set between them. Rowler led the others in a makeshift game of trapshooting. One of his thugs threw jars of honey into the air and they took turns shooting at them with their pistols until the jars flung their golden guts far and wide.

I had a need to relieve myself, which I certainly didn't want to do right there in the deadfall where I'd have to sit in it. But there was no way to climb out without giving myself away. A good hour later, when I couldn't hold in my pee anymore, Rowler finally padlocked the store, taped a sign to its front door and summoned his goons. He paused before he left the porch like he'd lost a thought and then found it again. He used his pistol's grip to break the front door's window glass next to the doorknob.

I waited until the dust cleared behind their trucks before I came out. I must have passed water for five minutes. Once I was through, I made my way to Rowler's sign. It read, "Building and all contents herein are the property of the United States Government as conveyed by the Commonwealth of Virginia. Trespassers will be prosecuted to the full extent of the law." I don't know what possessed me, but instead of hightailing it out of there I stood with my face pressed against the part of the door's window glass that wasn't broken. I could see inside the store and I can tell you a tornado couldn't have done more damage than Rowler and his men. The glass cases were broken and most of the provisions had been swept from their shelves onto the floor. Somebody had flung white flour far and wide from its canisters, a snowy dusting over havoc wreaked. Those men probably tore the place apart looking for hidden money and liquor. I'll bet Rowler was hoping for a stash of girlie magazines. I don't think Hiram thought about sex after his wife died, so he wouldn't have had much need for those.

If I knew Rowler (and at this point I think it's fair to say I did, almost too well), he broke that window so he could say Hollow folks raided the store and made that mess. But nobody with any sense would ever believe Hollow folks would rip up their own store and waste twenty-five cent jars of perfectly good honey in a shooting match.

I knew I'd been at the store's window too long. I'd just about managed to pull myself from it when a man's voice came from behind me. "You trying to get yourself caught?" I whipped around, ready to fight my way out of there if it came to it. I could only make out a silhouette at first, black as the Styx with the setting sun's glare behind it. When he stepped toward me, I saw that it was Torch.

"Bee," he said, "You done lost your mind hanging around here in the open like this?"

"Never you mind what I've lost, Daniel MacArthur," I said. I hadn't called Torch by his Christian name in a sow's age. He cocked his head, puzzled. He got more puzzled when I jumped him and hugged his neck like he was home from the wars. We were so tight against each other I could feel his heart beat in my own chest. It was right then I caught on to what Ruth and my heart already knew. I loved Daniel "Torch" MacArthur. I loved him something fierce.

I had sense enough not to say it right then. His face was about as long as a yard stick. I felt sure he was in no mood to hear my revelation. Most every bone in my body wanted him to know. It was all I could do not to pull him up the stairs to his old room and tangle my arms and legs up with his. Instead I said I was tickled to death to see him.

"We got to get you hid," he said. "Rowler and those government assholes'll be back. I'd stake my life on it. I'll take you down to our shitty new place." I leaned in to kiss his cheek. He kept right on talking and didn't notice me. His mind was on his Daddy. "Dad got real downhearted soon as we stepped through the front door. He can't feel Mama in it is what's the problem. I don't know how to make things right for him. I thought maybe if I could bring some more of our stuff from here it would help. I been around the bend an eternity waiting to see Rowler's taillights. Thank God Almighty they didn't burn the place down."

He led me up the stairs, but not the way I'd hoped. "Don't let grass grow under your feet, girl. C'mon. Grab that chair."

We carried two loads to where Torch hid his Daddy's truck. Then Torch got his heart dead set on getting their beds out too. I told him we might could lug the mattresses, but it'd be a cold day in hell before I heaved those chestnut headboards down the stairs. "We've carried out all we can," I said. "A headboard isn't gonna fix what's wrong with your Daddy."

Torch took a seat on his mattress. He looked stunned, like maybe he'd just figured out he and his Daddy wouldn't lay their heads down in their real home ever again. I sat down beside him and took his hand. He stared straight ahead. In his head he was looking in the windows of that new resettlement house, watching his Daddy pace the rooms, lost.

I gathered up enough courage to say "I love you."

"I know," he said. "Me too." See, we'd declared our love plenty. Brotherly, sisterly love. This was different. I needed to get it through his thick skull.

"Torch, you idiot. I'm trying to tell you I'm in love with you. Grown-up love. You'd better do something about it before I change my mind."

He turned toward me slowly, like his neck was a spit and his head the roast. He blinked away that sad picture he'd had his eyes on and saw me for the first time that day. All he could say was "huh?"

"Oh Jesus H. Christ," I said, and kissed him hard on the mouth.

I was beginning to think I'd have to draw him a map. Well, soon as I kissed him he found his way just fine all on his own. We were both of us in a fever. We said things without words. At the end of it he told me, through closed lips, that he was mine.

We fell asleep as two lovers, his arms a cloak around me. I woke to the sound of Torch cursing up a storm. "Shit," he said. "Shit, goddammit all to hell. Bee, wake up."

"I'm awake," I said. "What the hell is wrong with you?"

"We've been asleep for hours. Look outside. It's dark."

I told him to relax. Rowler'd already taken what he wanted. He wasn't coming back. Soon as I got the words out, it was my turn to cuss. I heard the store's front door jingle open, then Rowler's boot steps. I was sure it was him. I would know that bastard was in a room even if I was hog-tied, blindfolded and had my head sunk in a bucket of molasses. Another pair of feet followed after Rowler, probably that Ten-Dollar Whitman fellow.

We didn't dare move for fear the sound would give us away. We were quite a sight I'm sure -- two mostly-naked fools, stunned still before we could pull our pants up. We listened for Rowler's boots on the stairs. They never came that far, just trudged around downstairs for a while, then left. We could hear him outside half-snarling, half-laughing it up. Doing bad sure did warm the cockles of that man's heart. I wondered if he prayed for war and pestilence before bed at night. I was beginning to wonder why he was lollygagging around outside when I smelled fire. Torch smelled it too. He ducked down the stairs before I could stop him, the flames his very own Pied Piper. I caught up with him at the bottom. The blaze had put up a wall in front of us. Maybe he saw his mama in it, I don't know, but if I hadn't been there to stop him I swear Torch would have walked right into it.

I had to say his name twice and grab his arm to wake him from his trance. He followed me back up the stairs, out the window and down the backyard sycamore tree. Rowler and Whitman were out front, so they didn't see our escape. We beat it out of there fast. I made sure Torch didn't look back.

Torch wanted me to go with him to his daddy's government house. It took me a while to talk him out of it. I managed to convince him to let me go back to the snakes' cave. "I left all the money we saved up there," I said.

"It ain't worth you getting caught," he said.

"I won't. Ruth's last letter to me is up there too."

"I'll go get it. I can't take a chance on losing you." Torch pulled me to him like he'd done it a thousand times. We were new lovers, fresh picked. Yet somehow he already knew the places on me where his hands fit. I can't explain why it felt ordinary to be with him that way. It did, in the most impossible, wonderful way.

"You can't go," I said. "You'll never find where I hid it."

"Then I'll go with you."

I could see it wasn't going to be easy to get him to let me go. I had a bad need to go alone. There was a job needed doing that only I could do. So I told Torch I wanted to say goodbye to Daddy one last time. I told him I wanted to do it by myself, just me and Daddy. That he understood. He gave me a day. Said he'd be back to pick me up the next night. That was all the time I needed to take care of my business with Rowler.

| LEADING ROWLER TO A TRAP |

I spent the better part of the next day in search of Rowler. Didn't it figure he was everywhere when I was looking to avoid him, but nowhere when I wanted him? I finally spotted a mass of smoke and went towards it. Rowler and his men burned down every home, barn and chicken coop they came across, as if our humble cabins were a blight on the natural scenery. Ridding the mountain of them was one way to be sure we couldn't come back.

This time it was Red's place. His house was as much trickster as its owner -- the boards scorched black but didn't burn through. From a distance, I could see Ten-Dollar Whitman douse the place with enough kerosene to light up all of Ragged Mountain. Lucky for those idiots and the rest of us, lazy Red's yard was nothing but a ribbon of dirt too wide for the flames to jump.

I came across Red hiding in a pine twenty yards from his place. I heard a quiet whistle when I walked underneath it. His ass was planted on a thick branch halfway up. I climbed up to meet him.

"You'd best git girl," he said. "Them government assholes been looking for you are over at my place."

"I know." I looked toward Red's house, swallowed by smoke. I told Red I was sorry.

"Yeah. Me too."

We linked hands, him on a higher branch and me on the one beneath. We stared at the fire. The sound of his glass windows bursting broke our silence. Red took his hand away to wipe his face clean of tears. He said the goddamned smoke made his eyes water.

I told him I had an errand. "I'll see you," I said. I slid down the tree, headed in Rowler's direction.

"Hold on there," Red said. "What you fixin' to do?"

"Don't come after me," I said. "Swear you won't you son of a bitch."

"Jesus Bee. Torch'll string me up he finds out I let you do whatever the hell it is you're aiming at."

"Then don't tell him you saw me, dummy. You follow me you're going to get yourself shot, then Torch'll kill me."

Red knew me well enough to know when there was no reasoning with me. "Go on with you then," he said.

I spied on Rowler from the trees first. I ran through my plan in my head. I drew in a deep breath, then I ran right for him. The sound of me coming startled him. He spun around to face me. I darted to his right. He was so surprised at first he didn't move, then his feet caught on and came after me. He shouted, "Whitman! C'mon! It's that little bitch."

Rowler was too close. I needed to put some air between us, so I ran straight up the mountain. It was a trudge for Hollow folk, near impossible for level landers like Rowler and his man Whitman to take at more than a stroll. It worked. Rowler was about fifty paces behind, Whitman another twenty five behind him.

I cut across what was left of Watson's farm, which wasn't much since Rowler and Whitman had been there with their kerosene can. I sloshed through Brokenback. The water's drag slowed me enough that Rowler was on me again, but then it slowed him too and I pulled away. I cleared a downed tree stump only to get grabbed by a briar bush on the other side and laid out flat. I was up quick as you please, but my left knee hurt something fierce. I willed my legs to move fast as they'd ever gone. I'd almost made it. Now was when speed counted the most.

I dashed into Outlaw Jones' yard. As I'd hoped, the dogs were sleeping in the cool shade under the house. By the time they got up and raised the alarm, I was clear across the front of the property. I scrambled up a tree in time to watch Rowler charge onto Jones' place, sidearm drawn. The dogs pounced on him. Rowler shot a red coonhound that had a hold of his leg. That's when all hell broke loose.

The muzzles of two shotguns and one rifle blasted Rowler from the cabin's two open windows. The lead shotgun pellets hit him first. His torso jerked backward, first on his right side -- where little red spots grew on his shoulder -- then on his left at his bloodied belt line. He got off two shots from his pistol before a rifle cartridge went through his temple sideways and took the crown of his head with it.

Rowler's man Whitman had sense enough to stop back at the tree line soon as the shooting started. Far as I could tell, he got away without a scratch on him.

The dogs were in a frenzy, worked up from the intrusion and the shooting that followed. As soon as Rowler went down, they went to work tearing him to pieces.

The dogs otherwise occupied, I made my way down the mountain to meet Torch. I didn't tell him about the day's events. I didn't see the use in getting him all lathered up. Besides, Mama was next. I needed to plan.

| ONE LAST LOOK AT MAMA |

Torch fought with me again that evening, over where I was going to stay. He wanted me in the house with him and Hiram. I told him that was a one hell of a shitty idea. If the law found me there, it'd be Peter and Ruth all over again. Mules would have to sprout wings and fly before I'd put anyone else I loved in danger. Since Rowler wouldn't be hunting for me anymore, I figured it would be safe enough to hide out in the new chicken coop Torch and his daddy built that day. "You're not going to budge me," I said, "so you might as well give up." He did.

Torch carried me down the mountain in the back of his pickup, hidden under blankets and loose hay. After a bone-rattling ride over dirt mountain roads, the tires hit smooth pavement. When we stopped, he picked me up, blanket and all, and carried me into the goddamned chicken coop. It was the second-to-last place on earth I wanted to be (the first being back at The Colony with Nurse Chick), but I'd asked for it. I told him to get out and close the door. There was still enough light to see by. Mama lived in the house next door. The air was heavy because of it. The last thing I needed was for her to see Torch hanging out in the coop and get suspicious. Once he got the door closed, Torch whispered through it, "Bee, you okay in there?"

"Yes," I said. "Now go on."

"Alright."

I could tell he was still standing there. "I love you," I said.

"I love you," he said and went back to the house.

So there I was, living among the chickens some other Hollow folk had given to Torch and his Daddy so at least they'd have fresh eggs. Chickens like to roam when the sun is up, so I had the foul-smelling place all to myself during the day. Then Torch let me out at night so I could stretch the kinks out of my legs and breathe air that wasn't thick with downy puffs. You know how I feel about chickens, so you can guess my opinion of the accommodations.

Torch was ready to leave for the train yard that first night, but I told him he'd better get his Daddy settled in first. There was no sense in leaving with worry on his mind. Once he got Hiram squared away, I said, we could head towards our new life.

I could see Mama's house from my chicken coop. It was painted a clean white. The windows were framed by black shutters, each perfectly aligned with the others, straight across as a ruler. During the day, Mama worked in her garden. She tried to make it orderly. Its rows and sections were marked with twine, but the perfect lines and squares overflowed with tousled green leaves big as dinner plates, twisted vines heavy with cucumbers, and fat, round, red tomatoes. I couldn't see any weeds from my coop, but now and then she'd grab at something and yank it up out of her perfect garden picture.

Sometimes at night, after Torch freed me from my coop, I'd walk towards Mama's little black and white house while I thought on ways to kill her. One room on the inside was always lit up against the dark. When I got close enough, I could see Mama through the window. I stood unseen in the darkness and watched while she sipped at her iced tea and pushed her rocker back and forth with her naked feet. I always thought her feet gave her away. She'd have everyone believe she was Dickens' prince, only playing the pauper until she returned to her rightful place on the throne. She was so careful not to talk or dress or behave like the rest of us. But she hid peasant's feet under her shoes -- flat and broad, rough with calluses rubbed by walking and work. I remember her bare toes would twitch at night, after she freed them from their hiding spots in her shoes, jittery from keeping her secret all day.

After a week of watching Mama from afar, I was ready to get her good and dead. I just had to figure out how to get my hands on a gun. I decided that was the way to go since shooting was fast and foolproof. A gun was it. Hiram kept a pistol under the cash box at the store in case some randy out-of-towner got the idea he wanted that money for himself. It stood to reason he still had it, but I couldn't ask Torch. Soon as Torch came asking did I know Rowler'd gone and gotten himself shot by Outlaw Jones, I opened my big mouth and told him about how it was me who lured Rowler into his own deathtrap. Torch was entirely unsettled at the thought of me having anything to do with that bastard's death, even though he agreed Rowler needed killing. Torch was afraid I'd get myself locked up at the Colony again or, he said, someplace worse. I didn't tell him I was sure there was no worse place in the world. The short of it was he wasn't about to help me get myself into more trouble.

I needed a pistol. If I tried to walk into Mama's swinging a shotgun, there were all kinds of things could go bad wrong. The problem was not too many Hollow folks had a need for a pistol. The bootleggers did. I was sure Red had one. It was my bad luck I didn't know where on God's green earth he'd gotten to. Thank the Lord my addled brain remembered seeing one at the Acheson's resettlement house. You remember Torch and I went to visit them a few weeks before. I marveled at their electric lights. I knew they still had Grandpa Acheson's war trophy, that poor dead Yankee officer's Colt 44. I snuck down there right before dawn. Sam was fresh from bed, putting the coffee on. I managed to talk him into loaning me the pistol in spite of his nervousness about it. I told him I'd gotten Rowler killed and I was gunning for more government men. I knew he was more likely to let me borrow the gun if he thought I was going to use it to get back at the ones who'd taken our land. He'd never understand if I told him I wanted to kill my own mama and I didn't care to explain it.

I turned that Colt over in my hands all the next day in my coop while I waited for sundown. I rolled the bullets around my palm like two deadly marbles. Torch had already told me we'd leave the next morning. We had a duffel bag packed with clothes (I'd taken to wearing Torch's shirts and pants since my own had sprung so many holes I might as well have been in the altogether), some food and a blanket. I was going to wear his grandaddy's money belt, stuffed with every dime we had. Torch said some of the tramps might jump him for it but they weren't likely to roll a girl. With us ready to strike out, that night was my one and only chance to see that Mama got what she deserved. Come dark, Torch stayed inside playing cards with Hiram, which gave me the chance to sneak over to Mama's him none the wiser.

I felt uneasy climbing her steps, a visitor at her new house. Her door would be open. No one in the Hollow had locks on their doors. The government houses did, but it hadn't occurred to folks to use them. I swear the gun got heavier soon as my hand touched her door knob. I had it tucked into the waistband of jeans on loan from Torch. It near about pulled my pants down, even with a rope strung through my belt loops and tied tight in front as extra insurance. If that pistol was trying to tell me something, I wasn't listening. I'd come to deliver Mama's day of reckoning. Nothing or nobody could stop me.

I hitched my pants up. I left the gun stuffed where Mama wouldn't see it right away. I tiptoed through the dark in the direction of where I figured her bedroom would be. Before I crossed the sitting room, she clicked on the lamp next to her rocker like she'd been waiting on me. She said, "where the hell did you come from," which was about as friendly a greeting as I figured on getting. I told her about the hell I came from, told her it was a place called the Colony. I told her I knew she and Buddy had killed Daddy, except they were a couple of cowards who let the snakes do their dirty work. I told her as far as I was concerned she'd killed three people since Ruth and Peter were dead because of her. Then I slipped that two-ton gun (it got heavier the closer I came to using it) out from my waistband and pointed it right at Mama's heart.

Mama laughed. "You won't shoot me," she said. I told her I most certainly would. "You ingrate," she said. "I gave up everything when I had you. I could have gone back to Richmond, married a businessman. You stuck me here, with your stupid hillbilly father. I didn't kill him. Buddy did. But it was you who killed Ruth and Peter and don't you forget it. Rowler went there looking for you. If you loved them as much as you said, why didn't you find another place to hide?"

I went slack jawed. Course she was right. I never should have set foot in Ruth and Peter's house after my run in with Rowler. Then Mama said, "you think you and I are so different? You were looking out for yourself. That's all I've done. You were looking out for yourself, same as me."

So I shot her. I blew the toes on her right foot to smithereens. She had me right up to the point where she said we were the same. That's where she blew it. Blood and stringy bits of pink stuff that looked like bubblegum sprayed across the floor. Mama was on the floor too. For a good long minute she didn't take a breath, just grabbed at where her toes used to be and squawked. Then she commenced wailing and thrashing around like maybe she could wrestle the pain away. She cussed a blue streak. Nothing seemed to help.

I couldn't bring myself to shoot her again. I tried to do it with my eyes closed. I remember wishing I could cut out my own heart, since it seemed to be getting in my way, and just get on with it. She was too pitiful a creature. And she was my mother after all. It may not have meant squat to her but, even after everything she'd done, it still mattered to me.

That bullet she took to the foot was no small punishment. She either lost that foot or never put weight on it again. Either way I guaran-damn-tee you she was crippled. I hadn't seen hide nor hair of Buddy since folks landed on Resettlement Road (if I had, he would have been six feet under I can assure you). That's how come I knew Mama wouldn't have a soul to wait on her except her neighbors. Good, God-fearing folks she called mountain trash. Depending on them would be a bucket full of misery for her. I wish I could have stuck around to see it.

| GETTING A JOB IN THE CITY |

I sent Miles a letter all about what happened with Torch. I told him how sorry I was to throw him over. He'd been away so long and with only Torch to comfort me, I'd gone and fallen in love. The truth of it was Miles was too sweet-natured for me. A girl doesn't shoot her own Mama in the foot, then go home to a man who couldn't win a fistfight with a squirrel. Besides, Mama was half right about one thing. She said Miles should have come back and saved me from Rowler and all the rest. He would have done it if he loved me, she said. I knew he loved me in his way. That part was plain wrong. But he should have come back. Poor Miles just wasn't man enough to go towards trouble.

I didn't expect to hear back. I don't know why I had Torch take me to the Flint Hill post office, the return address I'd used, the morning we were going to jump the train. I wish I'd let well enough alone. Things would have turned out different for all of us. Wishing doesn't make it so, does it? So we went to Flint Hill and there was the letter from Miles.

He said he'd failed me and he was sorry for it. He understood why I chose Torch. He would always love me, whether or not his love was returned. And wouldn't we please go to Washington, since we didn't have anyone waiting on us anyplace else, and take his boarding house room for a while. The rent was paid. He wouldn't be back for a good two months. That ought to give us plenty of time to find work and a place of our own. Unless, he wrote, he could change my mind. "You mustn't begrudge me that." He liked to use fluttery words when he wrote about romantic feelings. "All I'm asking for is a chance."

I told Torch about the empty room. I left out the part about Miles wanting to win me back. I wasn't going to pick Miles over Torch. Torch was the one who carried my heart in his back pocket. There was no need to worry him over Miles.

So we went to Washington. Miles' widow landlady, Mrs. Martov, must have laid eyes on his recommendation of us before we jumped from the train. She welcomed us as long-lost friends and shepherded us up two flights of stairs to a gabled room with four windows. She had already dressed the bed and left a vase beside it with a rose from her garden. Mrs. Martov said it was a good thing Torch and I were brother and sister, since we were going to be in the same room and we weren't married. I agreed since it seemed important to her.

The view from Miles' room on the north side was the promenade that cut Stanton Park in two and passed by the stone figure of Major General Nathanael Greene himself, still commanding troops to stand against the British from atop his mount. On the other side, our windows looked into the neighbor's house. It was even taller than Mrs. Martov's. Rapunzel's tower couldn't have reached any higher. The houses stood close as corn stalks in a crowded row. Our first night, I happened to look over and see the next door lodger brushing his teeth at a basin. If his window had been open, I could have reached across and snatched his toothbrush.

It got hot as Hades in the afternoon that summer. The sun baked the city streets, so that folks made a game out of frying eggs on them. They said temperatures hadn't been that high in as long as anyone could remember. Mrs. Martov used to take her long-nosed dog Sheba for walks before the sun came up. She was spared the worst of the heat, but she didn't always fare so well out alone in the dark. A man down on his luck ripped her pocketbook from her arm and ran off with it early one morning after we first got there. Mrs. Martov fought with him for a minute before he got the best of her. He gave her a black eye for her trouble. I heard her griping about him being a wop bastard while she sipped her afternoon vodka from a tiny, red glass (she said it was good for cooling the body in summer).

She got her cropped hair curled at a beauty parlor once a week. She was wilted as a cut flower out of the vase too long when she got home. In the heat, her red lipstick bled into the lines around her mouth and her cosmetic powder ran with her sweat, down her arched nose and jutted out chin, until it stopped to rest in the hollows of her cheeks and the folds of her neck.

The first thing I noticed about city women was how they cut their hair short and kept it in smooth curls or finger waves. You never would catch one with a mane as unruly as mine. They never left the house without coloring their lips red as fire engines first. They wore print dresses (instead of men's pants like me) with rows of the prettiest buttons I'd ever seen down the front or back or both -- which I didn't understand because any fool knows one side of buttons will do. I saw buttons shaped like every kind of flower I could think of, pearl buttons, even buttons made to look like tiny Scottish dogs. And the women wore high-heeled shoes no matter how far they had to walk.

My boss, Mrs. Bates, got after me to clip my hair and buy some dresses. Can you believe I found a job just two short weeks after Torch and I set our bags down? I could hardly believe it myself. I stumbled into it like a clumsy mule, but I couldn't have found a better one if I'd tried. I got hired to work at the one place in the world that had more books than even I could read in my lifetime -- the Library of Congress. It was much too upscale a place for me. I think Mrs. Bates just hired me to stop my loitering. I'll tell you how it happened.

The city was so hot when we got here, and with almost no trees for shade and no water for a person to cool their feet in, except what came from fancy statue fountains. Don't worry. I knew better than to wade into a city fountain. I did follow the sound of one until I ended up face-to-face with a bronze Poseidon, sitting atop a fountain gurgling with water I so desperately wanted to bathe in. He was surrounded by frolicking nymphs and lesser sea gods, the whole lot of them stripped down with not a stitch of clothing between them. It didn't bother me one bit, but I thought city people seemed too reserved to be comfortable with all that nakedness. For my part, I wondered if the figures came alive at night and had their way with each other.

That day in the heat, a man sweaty as me knelt by the fountain's edge and scooped some water to the back of his neck. "It's cool in there," he said. He waved his hand at a building that looked piped with frosting, like a wedding cake I'd seen on the society pages of the Evening Star. "I'm going in to hide from the heat for a while. Want to join me?"

"I can't go in there," I said. "I don't belong."

"Suit yourself," he said. "But they let everybody in. They have to. It's the country's library."

I waited until he climbed the front stairs and disappeared behind the double doors. Then I climbed too. He had said library, unless the heat had addled my brain to the point that I was mixing up words. I had to see if there were books inside. If they threw me out by the seat of my pants, so be it. I was too hot to care anymore.

Soon as I stepped inside, I saw what the man had called a library was nothing less than the most magnificent temple man could build. The Taj Mahal couldn't be grander. There were inlaid marble floors. A blue ceiling bowed skyward, framed by golden arches. White stairways -- more marble - climbed to the second floor, where stout wooden doors hid shelves and shelves of books. Anyone could touch the books, open them, read them. Someone took words from some of the books and carved them on the walls. "Tongues in trees," one inscription read, "books in the running brooks, sermons in stones, and good in everything." Another said, "In nature all is useful, all is beautiful."

I went back every day for a week. Mrs. Bates noticed me and, I guess took pity on me for my scruffy appearance, because she offered me a job tucking books back onto their assigned shelves. She said I had potential -- said she'd get me into school to learn how to be a full-fledged librarian like her. She even said she'd convince the Library to pay for it. I wasn't sure I deserved it, but I was pretty sure a library job and a life with Torch was what happiness was.

Torch got a job sorting mail, just like he used to do at his daddy's store, only now he was doing it in the U.S. Capitol Building's mailroom which was a right lot fancier than MacArthur's. They turned him down at first, but he learned from my loitering example and went back every day for a week until they let him see one of the managers. Torch convinced the boss to quiz him. See, if you named a major U.S. city, Torch could always, without fail, tell you its zip codes. He even knew some small towns, like Lunenburg, Massachusetts. The boss was so impressed he hired Torch on the spot. Torch worked the evening shift sorting mail, but the higher-ups started talking promotion right away.

We started to enjoy the city. We were vexed by it sometimes too. There was the hustle and bustle of people and taxis and that sort of thing during the day, but in the wee morning hours after the night's revelry ended, there was almost no sound. The Hollow always buzzed that time of morning, when I'd first get up to start chores. It beat with birds' wings and hummed in the morning breeze. And the bugs. Come summer, country crickets played a rousing tune until dawn. It seemed there were no crickets in the city, least not enough to add up to anything.

TORCH GETS FIRED AND THINGS TAKE A TURN FOR THE WORSE

A boy who worked alongside Torch in the Capitol mailroom was stealing stamps. Most of the outgoing mail got run through a postage meter. The stamps were on hand in case it jammed, which happened from time to time. The kid was just fifteen. His daddy was some big shot Congressman from up north. That's how come he got the job. Torch caught him red-handed. The kid begged him not to tell the bosses, said he'd gotten into a few scrapes back home and his daddy was going to send him to reform school if he made any more trouble. Torch said he wouldn't rat him out, as long as the kid returned what he took.

"Return it? I already sold most of what I took to a newsstand on Constitution," the kid said. "Guy there buys 'em from me for a penny each. Throws in a few girlie magazines too."

Torch told the kid he'd better figure out a way to buy the stamps back or put cash in the stamp cabinet. Either way, he needed to settle up and fast. The kid settled up alright. He took another couple hundred stamps from the cabinet and hid them in Torch's supper pail. He turned Torch in to the supervisor, who found those stamps right there next to his bologna sandwich and that was that. I asked Torch did he try to explain. He said there was no use. It didn't take a genius to figure out nobody was going to believe a hillbilly over a Congressman's son.

It wasn't much later that I got myself fired too, so Torch and I were both out of a paycheck. My boss Mrs. Bates liked me, but circumstances forced her hand. I'd been feeling sick for a week or two. I'd seen what Ruth's morning sickness looked like and my monthly was late, so I knew I was in a family way. I managed to hide it from Torch since the worst of the retching was when I was at work during the day. I thought I was hiding it from Mrs. Bates too. Turns out I wasn't as crafty as I'd hoped.

She told me one morning she'd baked me a pie. She said to come with her to the break kitchen and she'd cut me a slice. I hardly felt like eating, but I figured I could choke a piece of cherry pie down to keep her from guessing my secret. But when she unwrapped her creation, it was no fruit pie. Half a dozen fish heads and tails, glistening in the room's bluish fluorescent light, peered up at me from the pie's buttery crust. "It's a stargazy pie," Mrs. Bates said. "It's very special. My mother's people in Cornwall ..." I'd held it in as long as I could. I was sick all over Mrs. Bates' very special pie. Those poor little fish. As if it wasn't insult enough to be cooked in a pie with their naked asses sticking up in the air, I had to go and puke all over them.

After I cleaned up the mess, Mrs. Bates sat me down at the break table and brought me some saltines and a Coca-Cola. "They'll help with the nausea," she said. "Are you expecting a child dear?"

I fessed up. "Yes ma'am," I said. "I'm sorry I didn't tell you. I only just figured it out myself."

"Is the fellow still around?"

I couldn't tell if Mrs. Bates was of the opinion I'd gotten myself wrapped up with a beau who didn't think enough of me to stick around and get hitched, or if she imagined I'd spread my legs for so many men I didn't know who the daddy was. I didn't care for either notion. "Yes," I said. "We were planning to get married after we saved enough money for our own place. We're staying with a friend now. I guess we'll have to head to the courthouse more sooner than later." I smiled to show I wasn't some trollop in trouble. I had a man who'd make an honest woman of me soon as I said go.

"I hope he has a good job, because I'm afraid you're about to lose this one."

I asked her what I'd done to get canned. She said getting knocked up out of wedlock was a good start. She used more polite terms, of course. I told her we could get married that afternoon if it would make her feel better.

"It's not me, dear," she said. "It's the higher ups. Pregnant girls aren't allowed to work here. You won't want to once you start showing anyhow. It would be vulgar."

That was my last day at the Library. I've never been back since. I couldn't bear to put my feet down on those marble floors again.

I planned to walk home. I didn't get very far. There was enough heat coming off the asphalt to make Lucifer woozy. I stopped by one of those water trucks they had parked all over town with pretty girls serving up ice cold water to cool the sweaty policemen. I was thinking about asking for a cup when my legs betrayed me. The goddamned Benedict Arnolds went soft and dumped me on the ground. Right about then, it hit me that Torch and I had no money coming in and sure enough a baby on the way. I sat there and cried until a policeman picked me up and dusted me off. He offered to call someone for me. I said no thanks. The officer, Smithey I think, perched me on the handles of his police bike and took off in the direction of where I pointed when he said, "Where do you live, sweetheart?" The breeze in my face was hot, not cool like you'd expect, but it helped bring me back to myself. By the time he got me to Mrs. Martov's, I could speak in complete sentences again. I thanked him. Mrs. Martov must have seen me on the handlebars and wondered what in the sam hill was going on because she swung her heavy front door open fast as a woman half her age.

She collected me from the policeman. I told her I'd been fired, but I didn't say why. I knew I could hardly tell Mrs. Martov the man she thought was my brother had stuck a bun in my oven. She poured us each a tall glass of vodka. I pretended to sip at mine. I was afraid if I drank it I'd throw up all over her sofa. Mrs. Martov told me to buck up. My sweetheart was on his way home. Miles had taken a job managing the prints and photographs section at the Library of Congress of all places. He was coming home to stay. We could get married now. He'd take care of me.

I told Torch that night. We had three days before Miles took his room back. I told him I'd lost my job. I didn't tell him about baby you just starting to grow. Not yet, I thought. He paced while I talked. When I finished, he stayed standing, leaning against the wall. He looked thrashed.

"Shit," he said. "I'll need a job before we can get a place of our own. There ain't a snowball's chance in hell of me finding one in three days."

I reminded him he'd found the first one in just a few weeks, never mind that he lost it. We could sleep on the Capitol's lawn for a few days. Plenty of other folks were doing it. There were a few nights that summer so ungodly hot, people left their houses and took to sleeping on the grass around the Capitol building. They couldn't sleep on their own lawns since nobody in that part of town had a spot of grass bigger than a postage stamp. I read in the paper it happened other places too. If folks had stayed behind closed doors, they might have ended up roasted like those poor stargazy pie fish. Oh to be pregnant and sick in that heat was its own special kind of Hell.

"That's all well and good if I find a job in a few days," Torch said. "What if I don't?"

"You will," I said. "You will."

"Bee, it's the depression. I'll do my darndest, but if I don't have a time card to punch in two days, we're leaving."

"Leaving? Where is it you think we're going to go?"

"Home."

"Home is a park. You got plans to join the park rangers? You know other men from the mountain tried. The rangers wouldn't touch them with a ten-foot pole."

"No. I know. I mean we'll go near about home. I could build us a place somewhere outside the park. Someplace set back out of sight, where we could run a still."

"Jesus Christ on a crutch. I can't go back there. I got Rowler killed and I shot my own Mama in the foot. You think the law is gonna have a welcome home party for me?"

Torch said nobody would know I was there if we picked the right place to set up camp. "I'll make the deliveries," he said. "You won't ever have to set foot off our land."

"Even if I wanted to be your captive," I said, "what happens if you get caught? If the revenuers find you with enough booze, they'll lock you up for upwards of a year. How am I going to support myself if I can't leave the house?"

Torch had an answer for all my gripes. His daddy would help me. We could grow a garden. He wouldn't get caught. I was tough, I could fend for myself. I didn't tell him what gave me the jitters was the thought of fending for two: me and baby you. I could survive hard times in the woods in my sleep. But what if you had to go hungry or you got sick? In the Hollow, we had a pack of people to lean on. This time, Torch and I would be all alone. And what if I got arrested, for running moonshine or what I did to Rowler or both. What would happen to you? In the city no one knew me. I was just some hillbilly girl in need of a trip to a beauty parlor. Back home, I was an outlaw. It did no good to try and convince Torch. His mind was set on going back home, even though home wasn't there anymore.

He tried. For me, he tried. But in three days, it was time for Miles to come home and Torch still hadn't found a job. He packed our clothes into an old suitcase Mrs. Martov gave him. He bought us each a train ticket. No more jumping trains for us, he said. We were going to sit on fabric-covered seats in the passenger car. And he'd saved enough money from his short time as a working man to buy us coffee in the dining car. He said they would serve it to us out of silver pitchers, with cream and sugar cubes on the side.

On our last day, I told Torch I wanted to thank Miles for what he'd done for us, and say goodbye. Torch said fine, meet him at Union Station when I was done. The train was set to leave at four o-clock. He'd wait for me on the platform. He didn't have to say it for me to know he didn't want to be in the room with the man I'd thrown over for him, the one who had a steady job in the same city that had ground Torch into meal. Torch was too proud a man to want to look small next to Miles' success.

I put on my best work dress for the train ride. It was a spruce green dotted with little red cherries. After I kissed Torch goodbye and promised to meet him in an hour, I helped Mrs. Martov make doll-sized sandwiches, each with one thin slice of cucumber inside and a tiny dot of cream cheese. She called them tea sandwiches. We made tea, too, in a gold urn she said her first husband brought from Russia. It was painted with red and blue flowers and looked more like something Aladdin would have rubbed than a teapot. I offered to pour her some. She told me tea was restorative and I should have a cup too. Then she walked me through careful preparation of her own cup, which it turns out was only a splash of tea, a dribble of milk and a whole lot of vodka. I sat with her on the parlor's red velvet sofa until Miles came up the walk.

I saw him through the front door's glass first. He was crooked and wavy on the other side of the panes, a mirage. There was a moment when I thought it might be Torch come to get me. But Miles was the one who crossed the threshold into the room.

"Back from the wars, are you?" Mrs. Martov insisted on getting up to shake his hand even when Miles told her not to. She stood at attention while Miles greeted me, her heels together and her arms at her sides. Miles was still holding his bag and standing next to Mrs. Martov, so he could only hug me softly from one side with his free arm.

We sat for tea and sandwiches. Every time Miles turned from Mrs. Martov to me, his eyes looked to be floating in held-back tears and his face took on a pleading look. Of course I knew what he wanted. But I'd given my heart to Torch. There was no getting it back.

At half past three, when I got up to leave, something strange happened. A heavy, dank dread swallowed me whole. Breathing was hard work. Blackness closed in from every side. I had to brace myself on the tea table, which caused the teacups to tinkle in irritation. Miles led me by my arm to his chair. I motioned for him pull up a seat next to me. I felt launched down river. His hand was my only tether to shore. In the middle of all of it, Mrs. Martov, made chatty by her second vodka, was telling us about when her third husband had his first heart attack. I leaned my head on Miles' shoulder. He put his arm around me from the side again. His grasp was a little firmer the second time.

We must have looked a pretty picture: him smart in his travel clothes and me all dolled up in my cherry dress, both of us sipping at dainty cups. It might have been nice if it weren't for the storm in my heart. The man I loved was at the train station, waiting for me on the number nine platform, holding a bag full of my clothes and his, all wrapped up together. I wonder if the train sensed his heartache, lowered its steps kindly to him, opened its door wider. Come aboard young man. Rest your mournful head on my cushions. I'll carry you away from this place and from her, back home where you can try again to claim some brand of happiness. At Mrs. Martov's, the pendulum on her towering clock wagged its brass bob at me, scolding me for my choice.

Miles asked me to marry him the next day. We went to city hall to do it. The building was near about as pretty as the library, decorated like a cake too, filled with marble floors and walls and a grand staircase in the center. It made me wonder how much money our government had that it could afford to spend such a pile of it on just one building. I wore a cream-colored suit Mrs. Martov loaned me, left over from her younger days. The skirt fit me then flared out a little below my knees. The jacket had tiny pleats at the shoulders to give the sleeves a little lift, and there were two pearl buttons at the waist. I got my hair curled at a beauty parlor. I'd taken to wearing red lipstick like all the other girls, so I put a dab of that on and rouged my cheeks with it too. Miles wore one of Mrs. Martov's dead husband's suits. It was black and fit him almost perfectly, except the pants were a little too short. All I had to do was let them out and press away the old crease and they looked as smart as if we'd bought them new.

The justice of the peace was longwinded. The ceremony took a good ten minutes. Miles didn't take his eyes from mine once the whole time. We had a couple of clerks as our witnesses. When it was over he kissed me hard and the clerks cheered. It was a fine kiss. It was a fine ceremony. I had the urge to cry a few times when I thought about how it should have been Torch and me standing there. I bit down on my tongue real hard and the sadness passed.

There are worse things than marrying a man you don't love. There hasn't been a day since we got hitched when Miles hasn't loved me with his whole heart. He's always treated you like his own child. I never told him the truth, and he never asked. There's a chance he doesn't know. But you were born a fat nine pounds just seven months after our wedding day and you're the spitting image of Torch. Even Mrs. Martov raised an eyebrow over her vodka glass when she first saw you.

It only took Miles a year to get to where his paychecks at the Library were big enough we could afford a small house outside the city. We found a place in Alexandria with a screened-in front porch big as the parlor and dining room put together. I first took you out there summer nights when you were a baby. We listened to the crickets until you dozed off in my arms on the porch swing.

Miles still drove the old jalopy he toured the country in. When he brought a new car home, I figured he'd drive it to work in the city. Instead he gave it to me. A birthday surprise, he said. It was a black Ford, same as Rowler's. When I drove it, I half expected to see that bastard's ghost scowling at me from the passenger's seat. Even that didn't stop me from driving it the four hours it took to get back to the mountain.

| GOODBYE |

It was about a year after you'd first set eyes on the world. Miles had a conference that took him away from home for a few days. I packed a suitcase for you and me after he left. We were on the road in no time flat. I went to Hiram's place first, waltzed right up to the front door like I wasn't a wanted woman liable to get arrested if anybody recognized me. Lucky for me nobody did, not even Hiram at first. It was no surprise. I had beauty parlor hair and a new dress Miles bought me. I looked more city than Hollow.

Once it sunk in it was me, he asked me all kinds of questions like where I lived and who put that wedding ring on my finger. I left you in the car with the windows down so I wouldn't have to answer questions about who gave you your beautiful little gypsy face. Then it was my turn to ask questions. I asked him about Torch. Hiram said Torch was making a damn good living running moonshine. He had a place south of the mountain, on a dead end branch off Weakley Hollow Road, across Cedar Run. Hiram said Torch came back from Washington real mad. He hoped I wasn't planning on pissing him off again. I said I wasn't. I'd come to make amends.

Then he answered a question I didn't ask, about Mama. He said she told everyone a drunk park ranger broke in to her house and tried to have his way with her. She got shot in the foot when they tussled over his gun. He got scared and ran. The police couldn't prove it, but she told her story to the Richmond paper anyway. The government finally wrote her a check to shut up about it. She got enough money to hire herself a housekeeper who came a few times a week and tended to the things Mama couldn't anymore, like the cleaning and the wash. Good for her. I was done with Mama. She didn't matter a hill of beans to me anymore.

I fed you some applesauce I'd brought from home, then drove the two hours to where Hiram told me I'd find Torch's place. I had to drive slow on account of the roads being rough as a washboard in places. All that banging around put you to sleep good as the porch swing at home.

I sat in the car outside his cabin, working up the courage to knock on his door. The whole way there I planned what I was going to say. Then, sitting in his yard, I couldn't remember a word of it. All I knew is that I had an awful need to see him. And I did, before I was ready. I spotted him through the rolled-down window, in the car's side mirror. He was dragging a freshly-killed buck by the horns, still loose-limbed and warm. Soon as he saw the car, he let go of the horns and cocked his shotgun in a way that let me know he meant to use it if he didn't like the looks of whoever'd come calling. I got out slowly so he could see it was me, then I moved away from the car quick as I could so he wouldn't see you. I wasn't ready to explain you yet.

He rested the butt of his gun on the ground, satisfied I wasn't dangerous enough to require buck shot. Aside from his trigger finger, the rest of him stayed stiff, like I'd come to do him some kind of harm.

"So here you are home again," he said. He nodded at my ring finger. "You bring your husband?" Hiram was right. Torch was pissed off, still. If I'd needed some rocks ground up, he could have done it with his teeth.

"No," I said. "I came to see you."

"Fuck if I can imagine what for." He spit near my feet.

"You got a ten pointer." I touched one of the sharp tips on the buck's horns. "Torch, I ..."

"Janie!" He hollered it at the house. The door opened like he'd commanded it to and Janie Johnson stepped through it. She was sipping at a mason jar a quarter full of what was probably Torch's homemade whiskey. There were curlers in her hair. She looked right at home. "Get on out here and say hey to Bee Livingston, come all the way from the big city." Then he looked right at me and said, "Hey Bee, you brought us any of that good smelling stuff city folks call soap? It's damn hard to come by out here in the sticks on account of folks here don't never use it."

"Stop it," I said, low so only he could hear me.

Janie came bounding up and hugged me. She laid her hands on all my new parts -- hair style, earrings, dress, shoes -- and let out a squeal with every touch. "Oh you look so pretty Bee! Won't you come in and tell us all about what it's like to live up there with all those rich folks? This your car? Your man must be rolling in it!" She looked in the windows of the Ford before I could stop her. "There's a baby in here," she squealed again. "Oh she's so fat!" She opened the door and took you out. She held you up for Torch to see. "Honey, we got to get ourselves one of these!" Torch looked struck by lightning. "Torch, you better say something 'fore Bee thinks you don't like her baby," Janie said. "I been after him to make me an honest woman so we can start popping out young 'uns too. If this angel's face don't convince him, I don't know what will."

Janie shoved you right in Torch's face. "Take her," she said. He did. Janie kept talking, asking me questions without stopping to hear the answers. "How old is she Bee, 'bout a year? You ask me they're babies 'til they can run 'round and string least three words together. What's her name?"

She was set to keep talking after that last question too, except you answered her. "'Melia," you said, since you hadn't quite figured out how to say the "ah" part that came first.

"What did she say," Torch asked. He was still holding you, one arm under your bottom and the better of his two hands under your arm.

"I reckon she said Amelia. Hey Torch, hon', wasn't that your mama's name?"

"Yeah," he said. He hadn't taken his eyes off you, like he expected you were going to blink out "you're my daddy," in morse code. "Janie, why don't you go brew up some coffee for our company. I'll see if I can talk Bee into staying for supper." Once Janie was out of earshot, Torch said, "She's mine." It was a statement, not a question.

I denied it. I wasn't going to trick him into coming back to me the way Mama tricked Daddy. Torch deserved more than that and so did you. He wasn't even supposed to see you until I'd had a chance to tell him I loved him and see if he still felt the same. In the end, it didn't matter. The moment I saw Janie in her curlers and heard her talk about starting a family with him, I decided to keep my mouth shut. Don't get me wrong. I wanted to say how hard it had been that day to stand him up at the train station. I wanted to say my heart hadn't beat right since he'd left. But if he was happy, it wasn't my place to break it up. And anyway, nothing had changed. He was still living outside the law and I had you to think of.

I told him I'd only come to tell him I was happy, in love with Miles. I hoped he'd find the same with Janie. "You ought to get started on that family she wants," I said. "There's nothing stopping you." I collected you and started the car. It took everything in me to do it. I could see Torch in the rearview, watching us drive away. I bawled until you said, "Mama cry?" Then I made myself suck it up so you wouldn't think the world was ending.

That was the last time I saw him. A while later, I got a letter from Hiram saying Torch got himself killed trying to outrun revenuers on a mountain road in a pickup full of white mule. He rounded a bend too fast. The truck mutinied, ran off the road and threw him. They found him, cut to pieces, twenty feet from where the truck stopped. Hiram said something else in his letter. Torch had been planning to leave the next day to come get us, you and me. He just had to sell one last load to have enough for a house in town, the kind of place he thought would make me happy.

· · ·

That's our story, Torch's, mine and yours, the best I can tell it. It belongs to Ruth and Peter too, and Geraldine. And all the folks who lived in the hollows before the government came and stole every rock and every tree. I made more than my share of mistakes in it, that much I'm sure of. But I got one thing right. You.

As long as I'm on this earth, you won't see the kind of hard times I did before I finished growing up. I'll see to it that you don't have to choose between love and living. I know I've made a good goddamned mess of things up to now. I swear to God, the devil and whoever's listening, I'll do my best from here on out to make you proud to call me your Mama.

| AFTERWORD |

This novel is entirely fictional, but it was inspired by actual events -- a shameful and still somewhat secret part of America's recent history. In the 1930s, several thousand people who belonged to a now-vanished Blue Ridge Mountain community had their homes and land taken from them by the governments of the Commonwealth of Virginia and the United States in favor of a national park. Some of the most destitute of these mountain folk, portrayed by their own government as simple-minded hillbillies, were institutionalized and some were forcibly sterilized as part of the eugenics movement of the time.

Soon after the federal government announced it wanted to open a national park on the east coast, a group of Virginia politicians and businessmen recommended a site in the state's Blue Ridge Mountains. Uncle Sam liked the idea, and so the Commonwealth of Virginia stitched together Shenandoah National Park from a patchwork of more than three-thousand separate swaths of land and presented the lot to the federal government.

When sociologists and journalists arrived to see the mountain people for themselves, they seemed singularly focused on the dirt-poor residents of Corbin Hollow. In their book *Hollow Folk*, sociologist Mandel Sherman and journalist Thomas Henry referred to "unlettered folk," living in "mud-plastered log cabins." They described them as "almost entirely cut off from the current of American life."

Visiting social worker Miriam Sizer's description of Hollow residents was equally ill-informed. Cultural Resource Specialist Reed Engle includes excerpts from a letter she sent to a local newspaper in his article, "Miriam M. Sizer: Patroness or Patronizing," as seen on the National Park Service's website. "Steeped in ignorance," she wrote, "possessed of little or no ambition, little sense of citizenship, little comprehension of law, or respect for law, these people present a problem that demands and challenges the attention of thinking men and women."

These misrepresentations helped the government market the proposed assimilation of these people into modern society as a humanitarian effort. So it was with the support of the federal government and the American people that Virginia seized the homes of mountain families, many of whom knew nothing of the proposed park until they received a notice to vacate that ordered them to sell their land for meager, Depression-era prices -- in some cases, as little as two dollars an acre. Some residents were deemed squatters and paid nothing because they had never filed deeds with the county courthouse and couldn't prove they owned their land.

According to Katrina Powell, an associate professor at Virginia Tech and the author of two books about the people who lived in Shenandoah before it became a park, residents were led to believe they could obtain conservation easements that would allow them to remain in their homes. Sadly, many of those who left willingly believed they might someday be allowed to return.

In her book *Answer at Once: Letters of Mountain Families in Shenandoah National Park 1934-1938*, Powell includes a letter written by mountain resident Richard Nicholson to Virginia Senator Harry Byrd. Nicholson writes, "a number of mountain people have asked me to write and ask you if it would do any good or be a chance whatever of the people getting their homes back to have petitions before Congress on the grounds that the mountain people was badly misled when they sold their land for a Park believing that they could stay there and not be forced to move. Almost every man or woman who moved from the Park would sign such a petition."

In the end, only 40 people, most of them elderly, were allowed to stay in their homes until they died.

The federal Resettlement Administration, one of Franklin Roosevelt's New Deal agencies, was responsible for relocating the community to one of seven resettlement areas in three counties where families could continue to subsistence farm and try to otherwise make a living. But resettlement housing wasn't free. Displaced mountain residents who didn't have the money to pay for it could apply to the state welfare department for a loan, but those who lacked collateral or a steady source of income were denied.

Answer at Once also includes letters sent to the Roosevelt Administration by mountain residents asking for jobs in the park. The government turned these requests down, preferring instead to hire outsiders.

That wasn't the worst of it. According to filmmaker Robert Knox Robinson's documentary, "Rothstein's First Assignment," and its first-person interviews, some of the poorest hollow folks were taken to an asylum in Luray, Virginia and, in some cases, surgically sterilized without their consent. Doctors at the Virginia Colony for Epileptics and Feebleminded used as their justification the eugenics movement theory that the poor should be qualified as halfwits unfit to reproduce. According to the film, more than 8,300 people were sterilized in Virginia. It is not known how many of them were from the mountains.

Today, there are nearly 100 million visitors to Shenandoah National Park annually. Many of them don't know that entire communities existed in those mountains, or that people's homes were taken from them by their own government to form the Park. I grew up in Virginia and attended public schools, but in all my state history lessons I was never told about the people before the park or the Virginia Colony and the unfortunate souls who ended up there.

Now you know the truth about how the park was formed and the inspiration for Bee's story. I hope you won't forget the people who lost their homes to make way for the Park. If you find yourself hiking Shenandoah's trails some Sunday afternoon and you come across the stacked stones of a forgotten chimney or a tombstone hidden in the tall grass, pause for a moment. If you're lucky, you just might make out the low hum of a mouth harp or catch a whiff of pipe smoke drifting on the wind.

ABOUT THE AUTHOR

Meredith Battle is a native Virginian who first experienced the untamed beauty of Shenandoah National Park as a girl riding piggyback on her father's shoulders. Since coming across the ruins of an old cabin, she has been taken with the mystery of the people who once lived there.

Before becoming a mother, Battle worked as a public affairs consultant. She currently lives in a small Virginia town with her husband and son, one Labrador Retriever, and two ducks.

MeredithBattle.com

facebook.com/AuthorMeredithBattle

WITHDRAWN